PUFFIN BOOKS

THE GNOME FACTORY
AND OTHER STORIES

This marvellous collection, drawn from thirty years' worth of writings, contains some of James Reeves's most heart-warming and enchanting stories.

Many are his original creations, such as *Rhyming Will* – the story of a boy who is unable to speak except in rhyme – and *The Gnome Factory*, where six life-size gnomes and a handful of cheeky orphans help to avert a robbery! Others are traditional favourites, retold in the author's own fresh and distinctive way. All are peopled by the greatest variety of characters imaginable: kindly old ladies, raggedy children, mischievous elves, clumsy potters, golden-haired princesses, lonesome sailors and many, many more. The perfect combination of James Reeves's magical stories and Edward Ardizzone's irresistible drawings makes this a classic collection and one that children will read over and over again.

James Reeves was born at Harrow, Middlesex, in 1909 and was educated at Stowe and Jesus College, Cambridge. He was married and had three children. He wrote four books of verse for children and also published many books of stories, several of which (like those in this collection) were illustrated by his friend and favourite illustrator, Edward Ardizzone. James Reeves died in 1978.

The Gnome Factory
and Other Stories

James Reeves

Illustrated by
Edward Ardizzone

PUFFIN BOOKS

Puffin Books, Penguin Books Ltd, Harmondsworth, Middlesex, England
Viking Penguin Inc., 40 West 23rd Street, New York, New York 10010, U.S.A.
Penguin Books Australia Ltd, Ringwood, Victoria, Australia
Penguin Books Canada Limited, 2801 John Street, Markham, Ontario, Canada L3R 1B4
Penguin Books (N.Z.) Ltd, 182–190 Wairau Road, Auckland 10, New Zealand

First published as *The James Reeves Story Book*
by William Heinemann Ltd, 1978
Published in Puffin Books 1986

Made and printed in Great Britain by
Richard Clay (The Chaucer Press) Ltd,
Bungay, Suffolk
Filmset in 10/13pt Times

Contents

For
Harriet Fitch
and Lucy Ardizzone

Preface

This collection of my stories of the past thirty years, illustrated by Edward Ardizzone, contains much that has been out of print for a long time. It pleases me to think of an entirely new generation of readers, to most of whom these stories will come fresh. The writing, which dates from my prime, is clear and easy on the ear, if only on account of my bad eyesight. It has been done, as it were, not by eye but by ear. In looking back on this collection, what gives me most happiness is that it brings to mind a long association with my favourite illustrator. Others of my books have pictures by excellent illustrators but I am sure no one would begrudge Ted and myself our mutual regard. I could not think of calling him anything but Ted, nor can I call him an illustrator without qualifying the word. He is an artist in his own right, and any author ought to be proud, as I am, to have his genius at my service. We have never quarrelled over our work, as some collaborators have been known to. Our differences have been minor and unimportant. He has occasionally done a drawing which has necessitated a slight change in my text.

One book here reprinted is called *Rhyming Will*. This was the result of an inspiration on Ted's part when he suggested that I write a tale in which the hero is unable to speak except in verse. I treasured the idea and let it ripen in the back of my mind until it could be harvested. The resulting collaboration was one of our happiest and has given much pleasure both to Ted's and to my family and friends.

If it is asked why we have had this special relationship, the answer is that we are basically interested in the same thing. Many of these stories are either folktales retold, or my original tales in the folk tradition and idiom. This kind of story is at its best when it is factual, not atmospheric. Ted has a special aptitude for spotting the pictorial moments in a narrative. He prefers a text in which the author avoids purely descriptive writing and leaves it to the artist to bring the action, the person or the scene to life. I gave him a lot of trouble with some creatures called *Prefabulous Animiles*, where his imagination was severely but delightfully stretched.

The first of my books to have Ardizzone illustrations was a book of poems, *The Blackbird in the Lilac*. The partnership has continued ever since with several books of verse as well as the prose tales here reprinted. Our latest collaboration is again in verse and is called *Arcadian Ballads*. Some of the stories in this book were dedicated to our own grandchildren, some now with children of their own. I hope, as I am sure does Ted, that they too will enjoy seeing once more these stories and pictures of their childhood. Perhaps our work, like the wine we both enjoy, improves with age.

J. R.
Lewes, March 1978

Rhyming Will

Long, long ago, in the city of Mulcaster, there lived a boy named Will. His father was a poor shoe-mender. He was a good boy and cheerful, but there was one thing wrong with him. He couldn't speak. Not a word did he say until he was almost seven. Then one day he opened his mouth and said:

'I see a man down yonder street
  With pies and gingerbread to eat.'

Everyone was delighted to hear little Will speak, for they had feared there was something wrong with him. They were all so surprised that no one noticed he had spoken in rhyme. That evening Will said:

'Now I have washed and fed,
I think I'll go to bed.'

At this they were all astonished, and they were still more astonished when Will went on speaking verses. Everything he said was in rhyme. On a fine sunny morning he looked about him and said:

'It is a merry thing
To see the green grass spring
And high upon the wing
To hear the skylark sing.'

But next day it was dull and stormy. Will looked out of the window and growled:

'I hate the stormy sky,
The black clouds overhead.
Roll by, black clouds, roll by,
Or we shall all be dead!'

I could tell you a hundred things Will said in that first week, and they were all in verse.

Now the people of Mulcaster did not like poetry. They called the little boy Rhyming Will, and made fun of him. Even his brothers and sisters laughed, and told him to speak properly, like other people. But Will couldn't. However hard he tried, he just couldn't. He became very unhappy. How could he live in a place where people mocked him? So one day he said to himself:

'In Mulcaster I cannot stay:
I am resolved to run away.'

He took some food and his little dog Spot, who never laughed at him, and set off on the road to London. About dinner-time a carrier gave him a lift. He handed Will a pie to eat, and another for Spot.

'Now don't try to thank me,' said the carrier, 'for I'm deaf as a post, and I can't hear a word you say.'

When they came to London, the carrier put Will down at Charing Cross. Spot barked their thanks, and wagged his tail vigorously.

Will went in search of lodgings. He found a friendly cobbler sitting outside his shop, and without a word took the hammer from the man's hand and finished the job. The cobbler could see that Will was a clever boy, so he offered to take him in and feed and clothe him in exchange for help in the shop. Will told the

cobbler he could not help rhyming, and asked him not to laugh.
He said:

> 'Pray do not laugh if every time
> I talk to you, I speak in rhyme.'

The cobbler didn't make fun of Will. They had all sorts of
strange folk in London, he said, and Will was no stranger than
others. In fact, Rhyming Will soon became a favourite in all the
city, and people would stand and talk with him only to hear him
talk poetry. Will was happy at last, and the cobbler was pleased
because people brought their shoes to his shop only to hear Will
speak in rhyme.

There was one thing the boy did not like – a large crowd. Too
many people together made him nervous. Once, when a specially
large number of people collected round him, he lifted his head
from his work and began to speak.

> 'Oh what a c-crowd of p-people I see,' he stammered.

Then he hesitated before going on.

> 'All standing round l-looking at me.
> I w-wish they would all go back to their homes
> And leave me –'

Again Will hesitated and then finished off:

> 'And leave me alone.'

Everyone laughed. Some rude fellows made fun of Will's bad
rhyme. The boy turned red with confusion and ran indoors. Even
Spot looked as if he was ashamed of his master and slunk away
with his tail between his legs. The cobbler, who had been standing
near and had heard everything, was surprised. This had never
happened before.

But the idle crowd melted away. Will came out and got on with
his work. He was happy once more.

Soon it was Lord Mayor's day. There was to be a splendid
reception. The new Lord Mayor was to entertain an important,
rich Nabob from India. Now it was the custom in those days to

give a feast to every important visitor; and the City Poet, whose name was Elkaner Settle, had to make up a poem and recite it to all the company. But this year, on the very eve of the great day, Mr Settle fell ill. He could not come to the banquet, and, what was worse, he had not made up a poem. The Lord Mayor was in a terrible state.

'What, no Ode?' he cried in despair. (In those days important poems were called 'Odes'.)

Then somebody told him about Will. At once the boy was sent for, and asked if he would recite an Ode at the feast. The Lord Mayor told him what to say, and Will promised to make it into a poem.

'Mind,' said the Lord Mayor, 'it must be a very special poem – an Ode, d'ye hear?'

Next day the Nabob was received with pomp and ceremony. He was given a magnificent banquet and various worthies made pompous speeches of welcome, which the Nabob listened to attentively. At last it was Will's turn. He looked pale, but he smiled bravely as he was set high on a chair for the whole company to see and hear. The Lord Mayor told the company about Will's gift of rhyming, and said he knew they were going to hear a truly fine Ode, every line rhyming smartly with the one next to it. Never, he said, had there been such a boy for rhymes. Mr Settle himself couldn't do better.

Then a dreadful thing happened. Will opened his mouth, but nothing came out. The people nearest to him urged him to start. This made him more nervous than ever. How he wished that Spot was with him to give him courage. But of course dogs were not allowed at the Lord Mayor's feast. At last he made a mighty effort, and spoke out clearly for all to hear. This is what he said:

'My Lord Mayor, my Lord Nabob of India, your Worships, Ladies and Gentlemen, it gives me the very greatest pleasure to welcome our distinguished guest from over the sea to this our City of London. I hope you will be as happy here, Lord Nabob, as you are in India. May you enjoy health and wealth as long as you live!'

At this there was the most terrible confusion. People cried 'The Ode, the Ode!' But not another word could poor Will say. He blushed scarlet, jumped off his chair, and ran out of the hall.

When he reached his lodgings, he told the cobbler what had happened, and how he had made a laughing-stock of himself before all the fine ladies and gentlemen of London. It was a mercy, he said, that Queen Anne was kept indoors by a cold, or she would have been there.

'Whatever will happen to me?' asked Will. 'Do you think I'll be shut in the Tower or have my head cut off?'

'Why, boy,' said the cobbler, 'you're talking like other folks now. You aren't talking in poetry like you used to.'

It was true. From that time on, though Will could make up a poem if he chose, he could also talk in ordinary language, like you and me.

While Will was still wondering what would happen to him, a

splendid carriage rolled up, and a dignified gentleman with a dark skin and a high turban asked to see the boy. To Will's amazement he saw that it was the Nabob from India. He was even more astonished when the Nabob handed him a purse with five gold coins. The Nabob told Will and the cobbler that he had been so pleased with Will's speech of welcome that he had come in person to give him a special reward.

'You are a genius, my boy!' the Nabob said. 'Everywhere I go, I have to listen to stuffy Odes in rhyme, as long as ten elephant trunks. I HATE ODES! If I had had to listen to one more poem after that banquet, I should have been ill. That was the best speech of welcome I have ever heard!'

'Hooray! Hooray!' shouted Will, and all the neighbours, who had come out of doors to see the fine coach, joined in the cheering. As for Spot, he wagged his tail and barked so loudly that he had to be given an extra juicy bone to keep him quiet.

Eleven White Pigeons

King Rex reigned over a country whose name means 'The Kingdom of the Valleys'. His Queen was called by a name which means Pink Rhododendron Bud, but we will call her Queen Bud for short. 'All my pink petals have fallen,' she used to say, 'and I am nothing but a withered stalk.' Nevertheless, she was not unhappy. She had an eldest son called Sparrowhawk, four other sons and one daughter; she would sit for most of the day on a sofa in the royal apartments with her silk embroidery, a bottle of smelling-salts and the History of the Kingdom in thirty-six volumes, of which she had now read twelve.

As for the King, he was kind to her and treated her with great respect, listening to her opinion on all matters – all except those matters on which he was advised by the Lord Chancellor, a tall, thin man in black called Crabwitz. Chancellor Crabwitz was a most useful fellow, sticking seals and ribbons on all the papers which King Rex could not understand, and saving him endless trouble.

For the King did not like trouble. He was over fifty years old and thought it was time he had a quiet life. He had thought it was time he had a quiet life ever since he was about twenty-five, and so he had had. For his was a peaceful kingdom. Nobody worked hard. 'Most people,' he would say, 'work themselves to death in order to become rich so that they can be lazy and not work any more. *My* people have more sense. They are lazy without going to the trouble of becoming rich first. So they enjoy life while they can. They go fishing, sing songs and listen to the band. Very sensible, I call it – don't you, Bud, my dear?'

'Well, perhaps you are right,' said the Queen, 'though what we should do if there were a war I can't imagine. We have no army, the people know nothing about fighting, and there are no stores and no guns in case of trouble.'

'But why should there be trouble, my dear? Nobody ever makes war on us. What is there to make war about?'

'The people of the mountains made war upon us in the time of your ancestor Felix the Fortunate. I have been reading about it in Volume Ten of the History of the Kingdom.'

'That was a long time ago,' said the King comfortably. 'They have learned sense since then.'

'I hope so,' said the Queen, 'though in my opinion nobody ever learns sense.'

'Well, my dear,' said King Rex, 'I have nothing to fear as long as I have a sensible Queen like you and a sensible Chancellor like dear old Crabwitz. An excellent fellow, Crabwitz. He signs all my papers for me. He plays a very good game of chess too. Each time I play with him, I only *just* manage to beat him. That shows how good he is. There is only one thing I don't like about him – his bony legs. What a pity he has such very thin legs and such knobbly knees. They really look quite absurd in black stockings. Where do you think he gets black stockings narrow enough to fit such thin legs? I just can't imagine.'

'As a matter of fact,' said the Queen, 'they are knitted for him by an old aunt who lives in a little room at the top of the west tower looking towards the mountains. She's quite mad, they say, and spends all her time knitting black stockings for her nephew and talking to her pigeons.'

'Pigeons?' said the King. 'Does she keep pigeons up there?'

'Oh yes,' answered the Queen, 'eleven white pigeons. She feeds them on crumbs and talks to them. You can see them fluttering round the windows at the top of the west tower on fine days.'

The King looked out of the window.

'So you can,' said he; for there, fluttering about in the sunlight, their white wings resting gracefully upon the air, were three or four white birds. How happy and carefree they looked, as they preened themselves on the grey stone sills of the windows at the top of the square tower.

'Now, Rex, my dear,' said Queen Bud in a voice which the King knew only too well, 'don't forget what you have to do this morning.'

'No, dear,' said the King. 'Will you stay and help me?'

'No,' said the Queen. 'I think you had better do it by yourself.'

And taking up her silk embroidery, her smelling-salts and the History of the Kingdom, Volume Thirteen, she went off to her own apartments.

The King told a servant to call for the Princes and the Princess. Now the eldest Prince, Sparrowhawk, was a serious, hard-working young man of eighteen, who was away at college in the neighbouring kingdom. He had been gone for nearly two years. But the other four Princes and the little Princess, whose ages were between sixteen and ten, were a merry, careless crew, who took nothing seriously and never seemed to want to do an hour's work. The Queen had made the King promise to give them a good talking-to. They were seldom all at home, but this morning a message had been sent to them and in a few minutes they all came trooping in, laughing and talking. They looked so full of fun that the King knew he was in for a difficult time. He managed to quieten them down, and then he spoke to the eldest. This was a boy of sixteen, whose name was Blackbird.

'Blackbird,' said the King solemnly. 'You are now sixteen. What have you learned to do?'

'Nothing, father,' said Blackbird cheerfully.

'Nothing at all?' said the King unhappily. 'What shall I tell your mother? She thinks – that is, she and I think – that every young man ought to have an occupation. Have you no occupation whatever?'

'He can play the flute beautifully,' said the second son.

'Really?' said the King. 'I used to be able to do that before I lost some of my front teeth.'

'*You* played the flute, father?' said Blackbird, pulling a flute from the pocket of his jacket. 'Let's hear you.'

'No, no,' said the King. 'Not now. *You* play it. I'd rather like to hear how much you've learnt.'

'Shall I?' asked Blackbird.

'Yes, do,' said the others.

So Blackbird put the flute to his lips and blew a merry little tune which set the King's foot tapping on the royal footstool.

'Toot, toot, too – tuck-a tuck-a tuck-a tuck-a tuck-a T A!' said the flute.

'You see, father,' explained the Princess, 'when he was born, a blackbird used to come and sing on a tree just above his cradle. That is why he is called Blackbird, and that is why he can't help playing the flute.'

'Well, he doesn't play it so badly,' said the King. 'Mind you, he hasn't quite got *my* touch, but he will learn. Now then,' he went on, 'who's next?'

The second son's name was Tortoiseshell, because when he was born a tortoiseshell cat used to walk about on the palace roof screeching and wailing in a most heart-breaking manner.

'What have you learnt to do in the course of your fourteen years?' asked the King.

'Nothing,' said Tortoiseshell. 'Nothing except playing the fiddle.'

'You see, father,' said the Princess, 'how could he help learning to play the fiddle when he used to lie awake at night listening to that cat on the roof?'

'There's something in that,' agreed the King. 'Let's hear what you can do.'

So Tortoiseshell put his fiddle to his chin, scraped a little to tune the strings, and played a tune.

'Dee, dee dee – deedle, deedle, deedle, deedle, deedle, dee,' said the fiddle.

'Not bad,' said the King, 'not bad at all. Mind you, I used to be able to play a bit before I got the rheumatism, and I could do a lot better than that. Still, he's young, and he may learn in time. Who's next?'

The next Prince was a boy called Bumble, because a big

bumble-bee had buzzed all round his cradle when it was put in the palace gardens in the summer weather.

'What can *you* do?' asked the King. 'Make honey?'

'No,' said Bumble, 'I can't even do that. I can't do anything.'

'Except play the bass fiddle,' said the Princess. 'He plays it beautifully, father. You listen to him. He can give you a tickling feeling in the ears. Just listen.'

So Bumble took his bass fiddle – what we should call a 'cello – which was standing beside the door, scraped a few notes to tune it, and began to play.

'Zoom-ba-zoom-ba-zoom-ba-zoom-ba-zoom!' said the bass fiddle.

'Not bad at all,' said the King.

'Did you feel a tickle inside your ears?' asked the Princess.

'Sort of,' said the King. He had not felt it at all, but he was anxious to say the proper thing. 'Of course when I was a young fellow, I played the 'cello –'

Everybody laughed.

'That's a rhyme,' cried the Princess. 'You must be a poet, father. You can write us some words and we'll sing them.'

'I don't think I could do that,' said the King, 'though when I was courting your mother, I turned out some very passable verses. However, we'd better get on. Who's next?'

The youngest son was a boy called Mountain Goat. When he was a baby, the Queen had not been very well so he was fed on milk from a goat that had been brought down specially from the hills. Now in that country a favourite instrument is the drum, and this is made, as everybody knows, by stretching a goat-skin tight across a wooden frame. So of course, when Mountain Goat grew up, he had learnt to play the drum.

'Let's hear you,' said the King.

So Mountain Goat brought out his drum and beat it with two drumsticks.

'Br-r-room! br-r-room! br-r-room – boom, boom-ba-room, ta-TA! BOOM!' said the drum.

'Not bad at all,' said the King. 'I've heard worse. You might be quite good one day if you practise. And now what about you, my dear?' he asked of the Princess, who was by this time sitting on his knee. 'You're only nine years old and I don't suppose you can do a thing. Can you?'

'I'm ten,' said the Princess, 'but you're quite right – I can do nothing, nothing at all.'

'Oh yes, she can,' said Mountain Goat. 'When she was a baby, they put her cot outside in the fine sunny mornings and there was a tree just beside it with a few leaves left which used to twirl about in the breeze. That's why she's called Autumn Leaf, and that's why she dances all day.'

'Oh, you dance, do you?' said the King. 'Well, let's see what you can do!'

So the Princess slipped off the King's knee and did a few turns just to make her arms and legs loose.

'I'll tell you what we'll do,' said the King. 'We'll all play together and Autumn Leaf shall do a little dance. Then I shall be able to tell your mother you haven't altogether wasted your time.'

He quickly went to his desk, and out of one of the drawers he took an instrument. It was an oboe. He put it to his lips and, to the astonishment of his children, played a merry little tune. He did it quite well, considering he was very out of practice.

'Wonderful!' they all cried. 'Come on, let's start.'

So the King and the four boys all began to play a gay dance tune, while the Princess twirled about on her toes, round and round, just like the autumn leaf she had been named after.

When everything was going well and getting really noisy, the Queen came in. So did Chancellor Crabwitz. His face was looking worried under his white wig and his thin legs were trembling with agitation. The music stopped and the Princess sank into a chair, quite out of breath with dancing.

There was a terrible silence. The Queen was sniffing at her smelling-salts. At last she spoke.

'Wouldn't you like *me* to *sing* to you?' she asked in a voice of frightful sarcasm.

'And perhaps *I* could join in with the bugle?' suggested Crabwitz.

'Oh, *could* you, Crabby?' asked the Princess.

'Be quiet,' said the King. 'He didn't mean it. He can play chess, but he can't play the bugle.'

He looked at the Queen unhappily.

'I'm sorry, Bud,' he said miserably. 'You are quite right. We *were* making rather a noise. I wanted to prove to you that the children *can* do something after all. They haven't been wasting their time altogether, you see.'

'Sit down,' said the Queen, 'and listen to me. If this is all you have learnt to do with your lives, you are an idle, good-for-nothing, ungrateful lot of children. It is most distressing. I imagined you would have learnt something serious; instead I find you fiddling and fluting as if you were the palace orchestra, which is paid to do all that. I don't know where we shall end, I really don't. You remind me of the family of your ancestor, King Rufus the Eighteenth, who joined a troupe of wandering actors and were all eaten by dragons. You can read the whole story in Volume Seven. I am utterly ashamed of you. I don't know what to say.'

Here she began weeping and everyone looked very uncomfortable.

'But, my dear,' said King Rex tenderly, 'there are no dragons nowadays. I don't think things are as bad as you say –'

'Fortunately, your Majesty,' said Crabwitz, 'you have one son who has not wasted his time. The eldest, Prince Sparrowhawk, should be a great comfort to us all. A serious and devoted young man. I had news of him only this morning. His tutors at college speak most highly of him. He gained ninety-seven marks out of a hundred at the last examinations. A very distinguished performance.'

This cheered everyone up, so that nothing more was said. The children went off to play with their friends, and the King settled down to a game of chess with the Chancellor, and the Queen sat on the sofa and calmed herself down with her silk embroidery.

A few months later, the King and Queen were having tea in the royal apartments. All at once there was a distant noise in the city, a noise of confused excitement. There had been a certain amount of commotion in the kingdom for some days, but the King had taken little notice. He had mentioned it to Crabwitz, but Crabwitz had said there was nothing wrong, and that was good enough for the King.

Now, however, the noise became so loud that even the King could not ignore it. As it came nearer, he could make out the sound of shouting and marching, of a military band with drums and trumpets, and an occasional burst of cannon-fire. He went to the window and looked out. From where he stood, he could see the principal streets and squares of the city.

'Why, bless my soul!' he said to the Queen. 'There are men in uniform marching, people shouting and waving banners, and no end of noise and excitement. What *can* be the matter?'

The Queen came and stood beside him. Even as he spoke, a column of soldiers marched into the square in front of the palace. There was a mob of people shouting and waving flags. 'Long live the Kingdom of the Mountains, long live the Kingdom of the Valleys! Down with King Rex! Long live Prince Sparrowhawk! Long live the Revolution!' These were some of the cries which the surprised King and Queen heard amidst the confusion.

'Dear me!' said the King. 'Do you think the fire brigade is having a practice, or –'

'Don't be stupid,' said the Queen. 'This is serious. It sounds like a Revolution to me.'

'Impossible,' said the King. 'Why, we never have Revolutions in my country. Besides, Crabwitz would have told me about it. Where *is* Crabwitz, by the way? And where is the palace guard?'

He rang the bell and sent servants running hither and thither, but the Chancellor was nowhere to be found. Nor was the palace guard, which was usually cracking nuts and playing games in the courtyard with the children of the royal servants. By this time the mob was all round the palace and the soldiers were at the gate. A very fierce-looking general with an enormous black moustache hanging down over his mouth was sitting on a black horse shouting orders. He got off his horse and strode through the gates.

'I do believe he's coming in!' said the King excitedly. 'Do offer him some tea, my dear. I love to see generals with big moustaches drinking tea.'

'Don't be a fool!' said the Queen, who had turned very pale.

Just then the tall double doors of the royal drawing-room were thrown open and the fierce-looking general stood before the King and Queen. Beside him stood Crabwitz, the Chancellor, looking pale and anxious. His stockings were wrinkled and his bony knees knocked together. The general spoke. His voice was deep and ferocious and his great black moustache wobbled up and down vigorously as the strange words poured forth.

'*Boggl tanto, boggl carpo!*' said the general. '*Het noo marky marky het rumpf het bolgo! Twin iko bim hortico bim crampstok tot fletso punny-unny het bolgopuliat in WALLOP!*'

'What does he say?' said the King, looking round helplessly.

The Chancellor stepped forward.

'He bids Your Majesty good afternoon –'

'Ask him if he'll have some tea.'

Crabwitz ignored the interruption and went on. 'He is the general in charge of the army from the Kingdom of the Mountains. He proclaims a Revolution in the name of your son, Sparrowhawk, and calls upon you to give up your crown in favour of the Prince, at whose request he has entered the country.'

'Sparrowhawk?' asked the King in surprise. 'My son a traitor? Impossible! Where is he?'

At this moment a tall, handsome, young man with dark, frowning brows stepped into the room.

'I am no traitor, Your Majesty,' he said stiffly. 'For some time I have been distressed at the way in which you have ruled the country. The people are idle and foolish. The country is poor, weak and defenceless. I have come to govern. I will make the Kingdom of the Valleys a great kingdom. I call upon you to give up your throne.'

The Queen flung herself at his feet.

'My Son!' she cried. 'Can this be true? Do you mean what you say? Is this what you have been learning at college?'

Sparrowhawk pushed his mother aside roughly.

'It is no use, Your Majesty,' he said coldly. 'My mind is made up. The people are with me. The Chancellor is with me. I have the army of the mountains to back me up. You have an hour to make up your mind. After that, I shall take over the throne by force. I call upon you to resign.'

'Crabwitz,' said the King pitifully. 'How could you? Just when we were in the middle of a game of chess too. Who would have suspected *you*?'

'I am sorry, Your Majesty,' said Crabwitz stiffly. 'I had no choice. I did what I thought best.'

He said something to the general.

'Dohanyi bartok,' answered the general, clicked his heels, saluted the King and Queen, and marched out. Crabwitz followed.

'Remember,' said Sparrowhawk. 'You have one hour.'

He strode out after the others, leaving the unhappy King and Queen with two or three distracted servants.

There was a long and agitated discussion of what was to be done. The Queen wept and stormed, threatened vengeance, ran about the room and threw herself on the sofa. The King was very calm and cheerful.

'We must escape,' he said. 'We can't stay here.'

The servants told him the palace was surrounded. What would become of the King and Queen if they resigned? What would become of them if they didn't? In the end it was decided that they should try to escape into the forest, where loyal subjects might look after them till the trouble was over. The royal laundry van stood at a side-entrance, ready loaded with the palace linen. With luck they could escape hidden inside it. There was not a minute to lose. A few bags were quickly packed, and the Queen insisted on taking with her the silk embroidery, her smelling-salts and the History of the Kingdom in thirty-six volumes, of which she had now read twenty-one. They decided to take with them one old and faithful servant called Peter, and his wife Griselda. There was no room for any more. Two hampers of food were packed. Then the four of them crept down a back stair way to the side entrance. The driver of the royal laundry van was a coachman whose parents had been in service with the King for fifty years. He said he would drive them wherever they wanted to go, as long as his horses could travel. It was late in the afternoon when the van passed unchallenged through the gates, between the avenues of trees in the royal park and out towards the open country. No one noticed anything out of the ordinary. The escape, so far, had been successful. Presently, darkness began to fall. In a thick forest they decided to spend the night. Peter and Griselda prepared a meal, and afterwards they settled down to sleep.

'This is rather fun, you know,' said the King to himself, but he said nothing to the Queen, who was tired and unhappy.

They travelled on in this way for some days. The laundry van was not uncomfortable, and the two servants looked after the King and Queen as well as they were able. They saw very few people, for they were travelling through a lonely part of the kingdom. In a week's time they had eaten all the food in the hampers and had to buy more whenever they came to a village. They had forgotten to bring any money. The Queen had some jewellery with her, but it was difficult to sell jewels in country villages. Peter managed to sell some of the royal linen, of which there were large quantities in the laundry van. However, it was not easy to sell linen sheets and pillow-cases that had not been washed. All the same, they managed to get enough to eat.

The days drew into weeks. They had little idea where they were going. Nor could they find out what was happening back in the city. No one seemed to have much news of the Revolution. Autumn was coming on fast, and the weather turned colder. Soon they were obliged to light fires in the woods to keep themselves warm. The Queen complained of the cold. The old servants began to be worried. They could not go on like this all the winter. They would have to find a hut or shelter somewhere and see if they could make themselves comfortable. The two horses travelled well, but they had not enough to eat and soon began to look thin. Each day the travellers hoped to find an empty hut or farm-building where they could hide, but they had no luck. They dared not tell anyone who they were in case there were enemies looking for them. At one place there was a small company of soldiers who asked awkward questions and wondered why the royal laundry van was travelling so far from the palace. This alarmed the Queen, and at the next village she made the coachman buy paint and brushes, and he and Peter set to work to paint over the royal coat of arms and the name of the laundry.

The weather grew terribly bad. It rained without stopping, and it was very cold besides. It was too wet for a fire to be lit. The King and Queen sat shivering inside the van.

'It's no good, Rex,' the Queen said miserably. 'We must make for a town, and there we must give ourselves up, tell them to take us back home, and throw ourselves on our son's mercy.'

'Oh, I wouldn't like to do that,' said the King. 'We might be put in those awful damp dungeons with chains on our feet.'

'We might just as well be in a dungeon as here,' said the Queen.

'Well,' said the King. 'Let us give ourselves another day. If we don't find a hut tomorrow, or a friendly peasant who will take us in for the winter, we will do as you say.'

But he had little hope. The countryside was becoming mountainous and even more deserted. Rain was falling. Night was coming on. They were entering a thick wood. The road began to rise steeply uphill, and the poor horses were panting and straining.

Suddenly they stopped and pricked up their ears. A most unusual sound could be heard faintly, through the noise of the rain on the leaves. It was the sound of music – music and voices. This was such an unexpected sound that all five travellers, and the two horses as well, stopped to listen.

'People,' and the King. 'Undoubtedly people. What can they be doing shouting and singing in such a place as this?'

'What shall we do?' the two servants asked.

'Go straight on,' said the King. 'If they are friends we are saved; if they are enemies, at least we shall find out what is going to happen to us.'

The coachman shouted to the horses, which heaved and strained, and presently the van was lumbering up the hill once more. And there, for the time being, let us leave them.

*

What had been happening all this time in the rest of the kingdom, and what had been happening to the five other children of the King and Queen?

Well, soon after their talk with the King, the Princes Blackbird, Tortoiseshell, Bumble and Mountain Goat and the Princess Autumn Leaf had formed themselves into a troupe of travelling musicians and began to play at fairs and markets in the nearby towns. In this way they had earned enough money to keep themselves. The summer was fine and they lived in the open. They had never enjoyed anything so much in their lives. They played merrily, and little Autumn Leaf was a delightful dancer, so that soon they began to be quite well known in the small towns and the villages. There were other troupes of musicians and actors as well, for the country was very fond of amusements and dancing. Of course you may say it was a scandalous and surprising thing for the royal family to be going on in this way, but nobody was much concerned as to who they were. It is true that Crabwitz and other royal advisers occasionally told the King that something ought to be done about it, but somehow nothing ever was.

'Leave them alone,' said the King, 'and they'll come home as soon as the weather begins to turn cold.'

Then the Revolution happened. The army from the Kingdom of the Mountains marched in, the King and Queen fled, and Sparrowhawk was proclaimed King. At first it made little difference to people's everyday lives. The new King was busy arranging Committees of this and that. Then the Committees began to get moving. Sparrowhawk and his advisers had decided that the people were lazy and thoughtless, spending their time amusing themselves instead of working. So they made some very strict laws. One of these said that all music and dancing were to stop, except for a few special bands which only played in the big towns on public holidays.

All musicians were ordered to give up their instruments and get work on the farms or in newly organized workshops. Soldiers were sent round to see that they obeyed.

The four Princes and the Princess did not like the sound of that at all. They had made a good deal of money by the end of the summer, and with this they bought a caravan, a horse, a cooking-stove, and a great deal of food and warm clothing. They set off towards the wild regions near the border where they hoped to be left alone. As they went through the villages, they gave concerts and played at dances, so that they earned still more money to keep themselves through the winter. These dances were, of course, forbidden by law; but in the smaller and more distant villages little notice was as yet taken of the new law, and there were few soldiers to enforce it.

As they went they were joined by other musicians and by actors and dancers, jugglers, singers and all sorts of people who were off to escape from the new laws.

By the time autumn came, they had found themselves three warm, dry caves in the hills, far away from the big cities; here they all made themselves into a colony, working by day to make the things they would need, and singing and dancing and playing their instruments in the evening. When they felt it was time they had more money or wished to buy blankets or food, they sent out parties into the towns and villages.

The whole band – nearly a hundred of them altogether – were perfectly happy, and worried very little about what would happen to them in the end. They made Blackbird into a kind of Chief or General, because he was fair and everybody liked him. Besides, he was the eldest of the Princes, so it seemed right that he should have the leading position.

One wet evening in late autumn, soon after they had lit a huge fire in the biggest of the caves and started their singing and dancing, two men, who were returning late from an expedition, reported to Blackbird that they had seen a strange thing.

'A huge van,' they said, 'drawn by two tired horses, is coming up the hill. We did not stop to find out what it was, but came straight to tell you.'

A party was sent out to see what this strange thing could be. They very soon came back to report.

'A laundry van,' said the leader of the party, 'containing a hundred and forty-seven sheets, two hundred and three pillow-cases, ninety-six towels and the King and Queen!'

And at that moment the van struggled up the track and stopped at the entrance to the cave.

'Father!' shouted Blackbird, just like a schoolboy, quite forgetting that he was the general of an outlaw colony.

'Mother!' cried the other Princes and the little Princess.

The King and Queen, helped by Peter and Griselda, got down from the van, the coachman followed with their luggage, the horses were taken off and fed and rubbed down, and a wonderful meal was prepared by the cooks on duty for the day.

There is no need to describe that meal. No doubt it was not as good as the royal feasts of the old days, but it was better than anything the King and Queen had tasted for months. The Queen wept for joy; so busy was she embracing the Princes and hugging her only daughter that she could hardly eat. As for the King, he was too busy eating to embrace anyone until there was no more food. Afterwards he made up for it.

After supper they settled down to talk. The King told how he had been forced to resign by the wicked eldest Prince and the treacherous Crabwitz, and the Princes told what little news they had heard about the state of the kingdom after they had taken to their caravan and fled.

'I never did like the Crabwitz,' said the Princess. 'He was always telling me to go and brush my hair.'

'Yes,' said Tortoiseshell, 'and do you know what we heard in one of the villages? They said that his aunt, who everyone thought was mad, was really a spy. She lived up in the tower in our very own palace and sent out her pigeons with messages to Sparrowhawk and his friends in the Mountain Kingdom!'

'Well, fancy that,' said the King, astonished. 'The eleven white pigeons. So they carried messages, did they – and the old aunt wasn't mad at all. I might have known that a woman who knitted stockings like those wasn't to be trusted!'

The leader of the orchestra came up and bowed respectfully to the King and Queen and offered to play to them.

The King thanked him graciously, and the leader collected his players together. They performed some lively music, to which the Princess and several other children danced.

'Very enjoyable,' said the King, turning to the Queen. 'Really, my dear, you must admit that the children have made most remarkable progress. I'm quite proud of them. And of all the children, it seems to me that our own little Autumn Leaf dances with the most lightness and charm.'

Queen Bud smiled. For the first time for weeks, she was quite happy.

'Yes,' she said, 'if they had to waste their time, this is as good a way as any. And I must own,' she added, 'that Sparrowhawk has turned out to be rather a disappointment.'

Of course the King and Queen were invited to stay with the outlaw band, and they contributed greatly to everyone's comfort by making them a present of the royal sheets and pillow-cases, of which a specially appointed washing party took charge the following day. It was a little difficult to dry them in the rainy weather, but in time they were quite dry and even ironed.

The time passed happily enough. There were one or two alarms, but it was not difficult to hide the King and Queen if any danger threatened. Soon the winter came on, and the whole encampment was snow-bound, so that they were safer than ever. The King had brought his oboe with him and was able to take an honoured place in the orchestra, though it was not always easy for the conductor to bring himself to tell His Majesty when he was not playing in tune. As for the Queen, she had long since used up all her silk and finished all thirty-six volumes of the History of the Kingdom, so that she developed quite a keen interest in music. As a girl she had danced gracefully, and she was able to teach the children some new steps.

Then in the spring came the news that everyone was waiting for. It was a bright sunny day. A party had gone to the village for food, and when they returned they told how everyone was running about excitedly and telling each other the great news which had come from the city. The Revolution, it seemed, was over. Everywhere people were asking for King Rex back again. Bells were being rung, schools were closed, flags were hung from the windows, and there was singing and shouting.

What had happened was this. The army of the Mountain Kingdom, under the ferocious general with the black moustache, was very large and was becoming a nuisance. It ate up all the food, slept in all the best beds, tramped all over the place talking its strange language, and generally became most unpopular.

King Sparrowhawk summoned the general and told him that, since the Revolution had succeeded and everything was orderly and peaceful, he must take his men away.

'Sobranie poosgka,' said the general. 'Marky marky, het bojum, kodaly wopska!'

This meant that his army were enjoying themselves and did not want to go home at all. After that there were dreadful disturbances everywhere. People refused to give the soldiers food and the soldiers themselves became discontented and thought they might as well go home and see what their families were up to. Meanwhile, Sparrowhawk had been drilling an army from among his own people, and he threatened to go to war with the mountain people and turn them out. So in the end the mountain people were forced to go home, and the valley people's army was in charge of the country. Now nobody enjoyed these goings-on, because the valley people were most peaceful; moreover, they hated the new laws about working hard and not playing music or going to plays or having dances. So there was a new Revolution led by the important people in the army. They marched into the palace and took charge of Sparrowhawk and Crabwitz and even Crabwitz's old aunt, whose pigeons were considered to have caused a great deal of trouble. It was decided to ask the old King, Rex, and Queen Bud to take the throne once more – that is, if only they could be found. But nobody in the city knew where they were. Search-parties were sent out in all directions, and a valuable reward was offered to the person who should bring the first definite news of Their Majesties. Proclamations were proclaimed, and heralds with trumpets went on swift horses to all the villages and cities.

Of course it was not long before the King and Queen were found. The outlaws in the cave, as soon as they knew for certain that the Revolution was over, told the people in the village, and the people in the village told those in the town. Messengers came from the army, who were in charge in the city, and a bodyguard came to take the King and Queen back in triumph. A splendid red coach was sent, but the King and Queen said they would like to go back in the laundry van, which had been their only home for so long. Peter and Griselda went with them. They had fresh horses, but these were driven by the same coachman who had taken them away on the day of the Revolution. Behind them came the four Princes and the Princess in their caravan, and then followed the rest of the outlaws. Then came a host of villagers and townspeople in carts or on horseback. As you can imagine, they moved slowly. But how joyful everyone was! There was singing and shouting and waving of flags. The weather was fine, the birds sang gaily in the freshly budding trees, and wherever they went the children danced in the streets and the dogs barked with excitement.

There is not much more to tell. At last the procession reached the city, and the King and Queen and their children were back in the royal palace. With new advisers the King set to work – quite energetically for him – to put everything right again. The hard laws were done away with. All the same, people had got into the habit of doing a certain amount of work, and they did not go back to their lazy ways altogether.

There was the question of what to do with Sparrowhawk, Crabwitz and his old aunt. They had been thrown into the palace dungeons, where they lived miserably and uncomfortably for a fortnight. The dungeons were dark and damp, and full of toadstools, spiders and other annoyances.

'Put them to death!' said the fiercest of the King's advisers.

'Send them out of the country!' said another.

'Leave them in the dungeon!' said a third.

But the four Princes and the Princess pleaded with their father to be kind to them. They did not have to plead for long, because the King was a kind man.

'I'll tell you what,' said Mountain Goat. 'There's going to be a public holiday and celebration next Monday. Let the three of them out of prison and make them dance in the main square. Everybody will enjoy it, and it won't do them any harm.'

'Good idea!' said Bumble. 'It'll teach them not to try any more Revolutions and spoil people's fun.'

'A very good idea,' agreed the King, and all the advisers, including the Queen, were of the same opinion. So it was announced that on the Monday there would be dancing in the main square, to be led by Sparrowhawk, Crabwitz and the old aunt, who would perform on a special platform to the accompaniment of the outlaws' orchestra.

That scene must be left to the imagination. As you may suppose, the old Chancellor with his thin legs was no dancer; nor was his aunt; as for Sparrowhawk, dancing was not one of the things he had learnt at college. So the three of them were a very funny sight indeed. They caused much merriment and did not enjoy themselves; but everyone agreed that such a punishment was much less than they deserved for having caused so much trouble.

Crabwitz was allowed to go and live in a cottage in the country with his aunt, where she was obliged to knit woollen stockings for the children of the palace servants; but she was never again allowed to keep pigeons. One other change was made after the return of the King and Queen. It was decided to keep up a small army in case there was ever trouble again; Sparrowhawk was put in charge of it, and a very capable and hard-working general he made.

Now we must finish the story by saying, as everyone else did before they went to bed on that famous public holiday, 'Long live King Rex and Queen Bud.' A long time they did live, too, and the whole of their exciting and prosperous reign is well described – far better than I could describe it – in the History of the Kingdom of the Valleys, Volume Thirty-Seven.

The Strange Journey
of Tuflongbo

When I set out on my long journey, I took the south road from Shineland, meaning to pass by the country of the Picknickers who work in the mines. But I gave that up because a magpie I met foretold ill luck if I went there, and leaving that route, I turned off to the west, and travelled on till I came to the World's End, which is bounded by a high brick wall.

When I saw the wall, my heart failed me, though at that very moment I was on the very eve of the proudest day of my life! Over the wall grew a stout trailing plant, with a five-peaked glossy leaf and clusters of dark purple berries; and up it I climbed till I had gained the top, and through tears of joy beheld a strange country stretching beyond. As my eyes grew clear again, imagine my delight at seeing in the plain below me a vast body of men in blue aprons. What do you think they were doing? Cutting up the old moons and making stars of them! Yes, a band of men in blue aprons cutting up the old moons and making stars of them!

I was so lost in wonder that I remained for some hours spell-bound, and watching the process of conversion undiscovered; but at length one of the star-makers threw back his head, opened his mouth in a wide yawn, and I caught his eye. The only thing left for me to do was to bow low and introduce myself as Tuflongbo, the great traveller from Shineland. He laughed and yawned by turns, as he tried to repeat 'Tuflongbo', and then invited me to make a stay at his house, but I excused myself as I had a long journey to make.

At that, the moon cutters all threw their blue aprons over their heads and moaned aloud. So I hurried off as fast as possible, and travelled on till one evening I came to the shores of a vast sea, upon which no sail was to be seen. My heart sank as I paced the shore wondering how to cross the water; but at last I was relieved to see a lanky old man coming along with a bundle of nets in his arms. I began to question him excitedly about this strange sea and its far-off opposite shores. He did not seem to understand at first, but then he replied that if I crossed the sea, I should come to the country of the Applepivi.

'But how am I to cross it?' I asked him.

'Cross it? It is only three sights over,' he replied.

'Three sights over?' I replied. 'Will you be pleased to explain your meaning?'

'Only this: stand on the shore, look to the horizon, and jump – that is one sight. Pause, look, and jump again – that is two sights. Pause, look, and jump again – that is three sights. And then you are landed in the country of the Applepivi!'

'But how can I jump as far as I can see?'

'Nothing simpler. Just watch me, and you will be able to do it. I will jump across to the country of the Applepivi and back again in the winking of an eye.'

So said, so done! With one jump, he leaped to the horizon; the second carried him out of sight; and before I had time to cry out, there he was again standing beside me. I then shook hands with him, thanked him for his jumping lesson, took off with a mighty spring – once, twice, thrice, and found myself safely landed on the snow-white shores of the country of the Applepivi!

Yes – those three springs landed me sound in wind and limb on the snow-white shores of the country of the Applepivi, into which, before me, no traveller had ever gone. At first I could see no people there, but in fact the Applepivi had received warning of the coming of a powerful oversea leaper, and had retreated to their houses, leaving the open country deserted. But I found a beautiful tree near the seashore, on the fruit of which I supped deliciously.

This fruit was large and oval in shape, of a delicate brown hue and light as puff pastry. On breaking through the crust, I found the inside to be luscious, sweet and juicy. The fruit grew in clusters of four at the end of each branch, and some trees were so heavily laden with it as to be almost bent to the ground.

After I had eaten of this luscious fruit, a drowsiness overcame me, and lying down under the tree from whose branches I had plucked it, I enjoyed a long, refreshing sleep. I slept till morning, and then rose, wondering where I was. Near me grew a tall plant, like a foxglove with purple bells, and I picked one long stem. Carrying it, I took my way through mazy groves of fruit trees, and at last I came suddenly, in an opening, upon a cluster of round straw huts. Out of them poured swarms upon swarms of small people – the Applepivi, humming and buzzing angrily. I turned to fly for my life, and then thought better of it, and drew softly near them, holding out the stem with purple blossoms. After a moment of hesitation one of the Applepivi darted upon the stem and thrust a round little brown head into the cup of the flower; after which others followed.

Then I saw that this curious small folk had tiny wings under their shoulders and talked with a humming noise. The strange thing was, I understood what they said. They first of all asked me my name. 'Tuflongbo,' I answered, and I told them I came from a country across the sea called Shineland.

'Tuflongbo, Tuflongbo!
Back to Shineland let him go!'

some of them buzzed in my ears. But one of them, who had been buried in a purple bell, came out of it and said, 'Let us hear a little more about it, Tuflongbo. What have you Shineland folk got to give the Applepivi?'

'We can give you moors of purple heather and fields of bean blossom,' I said.

But the rest of the Applepivi only buzzed the louder:

'Tuflongbo, Tuflongbo!
Back to Shineland let him go!'

So back I came, over the sea of the three leaps, and over the wall of the World's End, and here I am.

The Old Woman
and the Four Noises

There was once an old woman living by herself in a little cottage. She was poor, but she had just enough money to live on, so long as she was careful. She worked hard, getting her meals ready, cleaning the floors and the pots and pans, and keeping her clothes neat and tidy. If she was ill, as sometimes she was, she had kind neighbours who did the shopping for her in the village, and cooked and cleaned for her till she was well again.

Her cottage was small, very small indeed. In fact, there were only two rooms – a kitchen and a living-room. She did not mind this at all. 'The smaller the house, the sooner it's cleaned,' she would say. Besides, what did she want with big rooms? There was a neat, warm stove in the living-room, with a hearth rug in front of it; beside the hearth rug there was a comfortable rocking-chair, where she would rest and read her newspaper till it was time for bed. There was a table and three chairs, a dresser for her plates and cups, and a few pictures on the walls. In one corner, away from the window, was her bed, for she had no separate bedroom. She liked to have her bed in the living-room. 'For,' she said, 'bedrooms are always cold and often damp.' So she was glad she had no bedroom. The windows of her living-room were low and small, but they looked out over the green fields where the cows and horses fed. There were green curtains with bunches of red roses on them.

The old woman kept no cat or dog, and she was not very often visited by neighbours and relatives; but she was quite content living alone in her cottage in the company of her pictures and dishes and chairs and all the things she loved.

Now in any house there are always certain noises, and the old

woman's cottage had its own special noises. When anyone came in at the door, there was a long, high 'Squea-eak!' It was always the same, just like that, a high 'Squea-eak!' and whenever she heard it, the old woman knew that the front door was opening. However carefully you opened the door, and however softly you let fall the latch, the hinges always made the same high-squeaking sound.

Then just inside the door there was a floorboard that seemed to say 'Creak, creak!' every time it was stepped on. 'Creak, creak!' the board would say when anyone came in at the door and stepped upon it.

If there was a little wind, one of the low windows in the living-room would make a rattling sound – not very loud, but just loud enough for you to know it was there, 'Rat-tattle, rat-tattle!' the window would say. 'Rat-tattle, rat-tattle!'

But the squeaking of the door, and the creaking of the floor and the rattling of the window were not the only sounds to be heard in the old woman's cottage. There was one more, and this was made not by the cottage itself but by something that lived in it. This was a little mouse that had its hole in a warm and secret corner beside the hearth. The old woman had never seen the mouse, and it never came out in the daytime, but she knew it was there; for sometimes at night, when she had settled down in bed and had not quite gone to sleep, she would hear a little pattering. 'Patter-patter,' she would hear. 'Patter-patter!' And if any crumbs had been left on the floor, they would certainly have gone by the morning. Sometimes the old woman would leave a few crumbs on purpose, though she knew she ought not, for mice were not supposed to be in the house. 'Nasty, dirty creatures!' people would say. But the old woman was fond of her mouse, though she never saw it, and could not believe that it was a nasty, dirty creature. She was always glad to hear the noise of its little pattering feet before she settled down to sleep. 'There's my little mouse,' she would say sleepily, as if it were quite an old friend. The window would rattle quietly if there was a wind; and in the morning, when she went to fetch the milk from the doorstep, she would tread on the creaking board and open the door. 'Creak-creak!' the floor would say, and 'Squea-eak!' the door would say, as if they were both wishing her good morning.

The old woman did not think about the little noises her cottage made. If she had been asked what sounds she liked best, she would probably have said 'The birds singing and the church bells on Sundays and the noise of the brass band from the village when it passes my door once a month on its way to town.' All the same, she would have missed her own particular little sounds if she had not heard them.

The nearest neighbour to the old woman was an old man, a carpenter who lived with his wife in the cottage next door. The carpenter was kind to the old woman, and helped her with some of the things she could not do for herself. One day he put up a shelf that had fallen down in the kitchen and another day he made her table stronger, so that it did not wobble when she had to cut a piece of extra tough meat. The carpenter had a little shed at the bottom of his garden, where he did his work and kept his tools – saws and planes and hammers and screwdrivers and chisels and all the things that carpenters need for their work.

*

One day it was very cold, and the old woman was pleased to see her good neighbour the carpenter coming down her path and past the window carrying a bundle of firewood. 'Rat-tattle!' went the window, for there was a cold wind blowing; and 'Creak-creak!' went the floorboard, as the old woman hurried to open the door; and 'Squea-eak!' went the door as she opened it to the carpenter. He gave her the sticks and she thanked him. Then he said that, as it was such cold weather, he would bring her some logs next day for her fire. The old woman thanked him and asked what she could do in return, for she did not like to take favours for nothing.

'Well,' said the carpenter, 'if I bring you some thick wool, you may make me a pair of warm socks, for my wife, though she is a good woman, is a poor hand at knitting.'

The old woman agreed to this, and next day about the same time she saw the carpenter passing her window with a wheelbarrow, and in the wheelbarrow were logs for her fire. She opened the door, and the carpenter began to bring in the logs, four at a time, and pile them up beside her stove to get warm and dry. As he did so, he heard the floor creak. Every time he passed over the board, it seemed to say 'Creak-creak. Creak-creak!'

'There's a nasty creak in that floorboard,' said the carpenter. 'You must let me come and settle it with a couple of nails and a hammer.'

'Oh, you mustn't trouble yourself,' said the old woman. 'I'm so used to it that I hardly notice it.'

'No trouble at all,' said the carpenter. 'It won't take me a couple of minutes. Another thing,' he continued, 'that door of yours squeaks. Nasty, weaselly squeak that has. I've noticed it before. Better let me bring an oil-can and settle that squeak while I'm about it.'

Just then there was a gust of wind, and the window rattled. 'Rat-tattle, rat-tattle!' went the window, and the carpenter said:

'Why, deary me, now there's a worrying sort of noise for a body to have to listen to, day in day out. Now, I'll just fetch a screwdriver and tighten up them hinges, and you'll never hear it again.'

'That's very good of you, neighbour, I'm sure,' said the old woman, 'and thank you kindly.'

She did not really want the carpenter to settle all the noises, but what was she to say? He was such a very kind man, and liked to take trouble doing things for her.

The carpenter had now piled up all the logs beside the stove. He was just going when he saw a little dark hole in one corner.

'Hello,' said he. 'That looks like mice to me. Are there mice here, do you know?'

'Why, yes, I think there are,' said the old woman, 'but they don't trouble me.'

'Nasty, dirty creatures, mice. That's what they are,' answered the carpenter. 'Just you let me bring one of my traps and I'll soon settle *them*!'

The old woman was just going to say she didn't really want to trouble him to set a mouse-trap, when the carpenter strode to the door and went out, saying he would call the day after tomorrow to settle all the old woman's noises.

That night the old woman heard the sound of the little mouse, patter-patter on the floor, and she trembled to think of it caught in a cruel trap; and next day, when she heard the rattle of the window and the creak of the floorboard and the long, high squeak of the front door, they seemed to her friendly noises, and she thought she would miss them when the carpenter had called to settle them.

'Well,' she said to herself. 'I'm an old silly, that's what I am. Of course my neighbour is right. He is a very clever man and he ought to know. They *are* tiresome little noises when you come to think of it, and I daresay the cottage will be a nicer place without them.'

The next day was colder than ever, and the old woman woke up not feeling at all well and coughing a little. She decided not to go out, as the wind was so cold; and indeed, the little window was rattling away as if it would fall off its hinges.

When the carpenter came with his tool-bag to get rid of the noises, as he had said he would, he noticed that the old woman was not looking well.

'I'll leave this little job till tomorrow,' he said, 'and send my wife round to comfort you, for it looks to me as if you ought to be in bed.'

Presently the carpenter's wife came round, and helped the old woman to bed. Then she got her some hot food and said she would attend to the shopping and do a bit of cleaning and see that the old woman did not have to get out of bed.

All day the old woman lay in bed. She was not very ill, and by the evening she began to feel better. She thought she would be able to get up the next day. But although she was not very ill, she was worried. There was something on her mind. Then she remembered that if she was well, the carpenter would call next day and get rid of all her little cottage noises and set a cruel trap for the little mouse. She told herself she was silly to worry about it, and yet she couldn't help worrying.

And as she lay in bed, suddenly it seemed as if she heard a noise of little feet. It was not the mouse's feet, but something heavier. Then there was the sound of a small squeaky voice, just like some other sound that she knew well.

'Old woman, old woman,' said the squeaky voice. 'Are you awake?'

The old woman was not frightened, for it was a small voice and quite friendly. Then she remembered what the squeaky voice reminded her of. Of course! It was the voice of the door.

'Who are you?' asked the old woman.

'Don't be afraid,' said the voice. 'I am an elf. You cannot see me, but I live in your front door and I bring you luck. Every time the door is opened or closed, I squeak just to remind you I am here.'

'Well, what an odd thing,' said the old woman. 'I never knew before that there was such a thing as a door-elf that squeaked, but now I come to think about it, I see no reason why there shouldn't be. Won't you come in and make yourself at home?'

'I *am* in,' said the door-elf, 'and I *am* at home. I want to have a little talk with you.'

So the door-elf told the old woman that he knew all about the carpenter, and how he was coming to oil the hinges next day, so that the little door-elf would never again be able to live in the door.

'That's pretty serious,' said the elf, 'and I do hope you'll ask him please not to do anything of the kind, but to keep his oil for other things.'

The old woman was just going to answer that she didn't know what to do, when there was another pattering of feet. This time a creaky little voice spoke.

'Hello, old woman,' said the creaky voice. 'Are you awake?'

'Yes,' said the old woman. 'Who are you?'

'I am the floor-elf,' said the creaky voice, 'and I live in one of your floorboards and every time somebody steps over me I creak just to remind you I am here. I want to have a little talk with you.'

'Certainly,' said the old woman. 'Come in and make yourself at home.'

'I *am* in,' said the little creaky voice, 'and I *am* at home.'

He too went on to tell the old women how he knew all about the carpenter and his hammer and his two nails, and how if she allowed him to hammer down the floorboard, the floor-elf would have nowhere to live and would never come back.

The old woman was just wondering what to say, when she heard the sound of more little feet, and this time a rattly voice spoke.

'Are you awake, old woman?' said the rattly voice. 'I am the window-elf and I live in your window, and every time the wind blows I rattle just to show that I am here. I bring you good luck and scare away bad luck that tries to come in at the window. I want to have a little talk with you, old woman.'

'Certainly,' said the old woman. 'Come in and make yourself at home.'

'I *am* in,' said the voice of the window-elf, 'and I *am* at home.'

Then the rattly voice of the window-elf also went on to say how he had heard all about the carpenter with his screws and his screwdriver, and how he was coming next day to fasten the window tight so that it would rattle no more and the little window-elf would have to go away and never come back any more.

The old woman was just going to answer that she would see what could be done about it, when there was yet another sound.

This time it was the very small pattering feet of the mouse. The old woman was surprised to hear the mouse speak in a tiny quavery voice.

'Hello, old woman,' said the mouse. 'Don't be afraid, and don't be surprised that I can speak. All animals can talk when there's something really important to talk about. And I have something very important to talk about tonight.'

'Welcome, mouse,' said the old woman. 'Come in and make yourself at home.'

'I *am* in already,' said the mouse, 'and I always make myself at home. Thank you for the crumbs you put out last night.'

'Oh dear,' said the old woman. 'That reminds me, I have been in bed all day and have put out nothing for you tonight and it is a very cold night for a mouse to go hungry in.'

'Never mind,' said the mouse. 'If you don't object, I will just step into the larder and help myself to a little cheddar cheese and two crumbs of brown bread.'

'All right,' said the old woman. 'But wouldn't it be better if you *all* had something to eat? Come along, boys – and mouse – suppose you all sit up at the table and have some supper. I'm afraid there is not much in the larder, but what there is you are welcome to.'

The three elves thanked the old woman in their squeaky, creaky and rattly voices, and began to help themselves. There was the sound of clinking dishes and presently the supper began. The elves explained that they were all sitting *on* the table, because they were too small to sit on the chairs. The mouse, meanwhile, told her that he also had heard about the carpenter and his mouse-trap and how it would frighten him away so that he would never be able to come again with his little pattering feet at night.

Just then the moon came out from behind a cloud and shone through the window of the cottage on to the table. And by its light the old woman saw the little mouse and the three elves. There they were, with their pointed caps and pointed shoes eating cheese and bread and pickles and a little cold sausage.

While she watched the supper party by the light of the moon, the old woman wondered what to do. She did not want the carpenter to come and settle things so that the elves and the little mouse could never come back again. But how could she stop him? If she told him what she had seen, he would just think her silly. She was sure he would not believe her story about the elves. So she looked up at the moon, and the moon seemed to be talking to her and telling her what to do. She watched it attentively for a few minutes, and then all at once it disappeared behind another cloud and the room was again in darkness.

'Hello, elves and mouse,' she called, 'are you still there?'

'Yes, old woman,' said the floor-elf in his creaky voice. 'We are still here and have just finished supper. A very good supper it was too.'

'Well, listen to me,' said the old woman, 'and I'll tell you what to do. Tomorrow my neighbour the carpenter is coming to get rid of you with his oil-can and his hammer and two nails and his screwdriver and his mouse-trap.'

'Yes, we know,' they said. 'Can't you tell him not to? You *do* want us to stay, don't you?'

'Yes, truly,' said the old woman. 'But it's no use my telling him not to get rid of you, for he is a very clever man and is sure to do it just the same. Now I will tell you what you must do. You must hide, do you understand? You must hide just for tomorrow. After that you can go back to your proper places.'

'That's all very well,' said the mouse. 'But what about me? I am always hiding. He'll set his trap just the same.'

'You must leave that to me, mouse,' said the old woman. 'I'll see that no harm comes to you.'

So they all agreed to do as they were told. The door-elf went and hid in a cupboard in the kitchen, where the carpenter would never find him; the floor-elf hid behind the old woman's bed in the corner of the room; and the window-elf hid in the old dresser that stood against the wall. As for the little mouse, he said good night to the three elves and the old woman and ran back to his hole behind the stove. After that, the old woman felt much happier and was soon sound asleep.

In the morning she was quite better. She listened to hear if the window was rattling, but there was no sound. Then she went quickly to the place where the floor creaked and walked over it several times, but not a sound was to be heard. Then she went to the door and opened it, but there was never a squeak. So she knew the three elves were still hiding. She got her breakfast and when she had finished it she washed the dishes and began sweeping the floor. No sooner had she started to do this than there was a knock at the door and the carpenter appeared with his bag of tools.

'Good morning,' said he. 'I am glad to see you up and better. Now I think we can settle these little noises of yours. Nasty, worrying noises they are too, but it won't take me long to get rid of them. Here we are! Oil-can for the door, hammer and two nails for the floor, screwdriver for the window, and – let me see, what was it? Yes, of course – mouse-trap for the little fellow behind the stove.'

'That's very kind of you, I'm sure,' said the old woman. 'But you know, neighbour, I think we must have been mistaken. When I opened the door just now to let you in, I could hear no squeak – no squeak at all. Just you try it.'

So the carpenter tried the door, and it was just as the old woman had said. There was no squeak, no squeak at all.

'Funny,' says he, 'very funny indeed. I could have sworn there was a squeak to that door when last I came here. Still, I'll just put a drop of oil on her hinges to make sure.'

'No, no!' said the old woman. 'Don't do that. Don't waste your oil on a pair of old hinges with no squeak to them. But if you could just put a drop on my big scissors, I'm sure they'd work easier.'

So the carpenter did as he was asked and left the door alone. Then he began to look for the creaking board. He stood on the board where the creak had been before, but now there was never a creak.

'Funny,' said he, 'very funny indeed. I could have sworn there was a creak to that board last time I stood on her. Well, she's a bit loose, so perhaps I'd best put a couple of nails in her to make sure.'

'No, no!' said the old woman. 'Don't waste your nails on an old board that has no creak to her. Perhaps you could put one in

51

the rocker of my chair, though, for it's getting very loose, and I'm afraid it may come right off.'

So the carpenter did as he was asked, and when he had finished he looked for the rattling window. But of course the same thing happened again, for the window-elf, like the other two elves, was hiding.

'Funny,' said he, 'very funny indeed. I could have sworn there was a rattle to that window last time I was here. Perhaps I'd best tighten up her screws just so as to make sure.'

'No, no!' said the old woman. 'Don't waste your time on an old window that has no rattle to her. But if you could just tighten up the screw in my pair of coal-tongs, that would be really kind.'

So the carpenter tightened up the screw in the coal-tongs, and then he got out his mouse-trap. He set it very carefully and put it down on the floor beside the little mouse's dark hole.

'There,' he said. 'I think that'll settle *him* all right.'

'Thank you very much indeed, neighbour carpenter,' said the old woman. 'Now if you'd like a cup of tea, there's a kettle on the boil here and it won't take me two minutes to make it.'

'Thank you kindly,' said the carpenter, 'but I must be getting on my way. I've brought the wool for my thick socks, if you've time to make them for me; for although my old woman is a great hand at a game of cards or reading bits of the newspaper, she's never been much of a one for plain knitting.'

So the old woman took the wool and said she would gladly knit the socks. The carpenter took up his tool bag and left the cottage; and as he went, there was never a rattle from the window, nor a creak from the floorboard, nor a squeak from the door.

But as soon as he was out of the house, the old woman went quickly to the mouse-trap and set it off with the poker, so that it would do no harm to any mouse. She made herself a cup of tea and sat down in her rocking-chair by the fire.

'Are you there?' she called softly. 'Are you there, window-elf and floor-elf and door-elf?'

She waited a moment but there was no answer, and she was afraid that the three elves had left her for ever. Then all at once a little gust of wind blew. She could tell there was a gust of wind, because it blew a puff of smoke down the chimney. And at the same time there was the sound of a little 'rat-tattle, rat-tattle!' from the window. Full of happiness and excitement, for she knew the window-elf was back in his proper place, the old woman went quickly and tried the creaking board.

'Creak-creak, creak-creak!' went the board, just as before. Then the old woman went and tried the door.

'Squea-eak!' it said. 'Squea-eak!' just as if it were saying 'Thank you' to the old woman for letting the door-elf stay with her and not be sent away.

So that is how the three elves were allowed to stay in the old woman's cottage as her friends; and whenever she heard the door squeak or the floor creak or the window rattle, she thought how friendly her little noises were and she was glad to have them to keep her company.

And at night, before she fell asleep, she would hear the little mouse patter-pattering on the floor, looking for any crumbs she had left him.

The Cat and the Mouse

The cat and the mouse played in the malthouse. The cat bit the mouse's tail off. 'Pray, Puss, give me my tail.'

'No,' says the cat, 'I'll not give you your tail, till you go to the cow, and fetch me some milk.'

First she leaped, and then she ran, till she came to the cow, and thus began:

'Pray, Cow, give me milk, that I may give cat milk, that cat may give me my own tail again.'

'No,' says the cow, 'I will give you no milk, till you go to the farmer and get me some hay.'

First she leaped, and then she ran, till she came to the farmer, and thus began:

'Pray, Farmer, give me hay, that I may give cow hay, that cow may give me milk, that I may give cat milk, that cat may give me my own tail again.'

'No,' says the farmer, 'I'll give you no hay, till you go to the butcher and fetch me some meat.'

First she leaped, and then she ran, till she came to the butcher, and thus began:

'Pray, Butcher, give me meat, that I may give farmer meat, that farmer may give me hay, that I may give cow hay, that cow may give me milk, that I may give cat milk, that cat may give me my own tail again.'

'No,' says the butcher, 'I'll give you no meat, till you go to the baker and fetch me some bread.'

First she leaped, and then she ran, till she came to the baker, and thus began:

'Pray, Baker, give me bread, that I may give butcher bread, that butcher may give me meat, that I may give farmer meat, that farmer may give me hay, that I may give cow hay, that cow may give me milk, that I may give cat milk, that cat may give me my own tail again.'

'Yes,' says the baker, 'I'll give you some bread, but if you eat my meal, I'll cut off your head.'

Then the baker gave mouse bread, and mouse gave butcher bread, and butcher gave mouse meat, and mouse gave farmer meat, and farmer gave mouse hay, and mouse gave cow hay, and cow gave mouse milk, and mouse gave cat milk, and cat gave mouse her own tail again!

The Gnome Factory

'I'm worried to death, my dear,' said Mr Turnbull to his wife as they sat together in the kitchen after supper.

Mrs Turnbull did not pay much heed. She had heard her husband say the same thing a dozen times.

'Have another cup of tea,' she said.

'It's not tea I want,' said Mr Turnbull. 'I'm worried, I tell you.'

'And what's on your mind, Harry?' she asked.

'Same trouble as before. I don't know how I'm going to make ends meet, and that's the truth.'

'Are there no more orders coming in?'

'Yes, there's plenty of orders. It's not that. Only old Pike has threatened to take over the factory and turn us out, if we can't pay a higher rent.'

'The rent's low enough, Harry. You've often said so yourself.'

'If I can't make more money,' continued Mr Turnbull, 'I can't pay more rent. And if we get turned out of here, I don't know where we shall go. We've been here twenty years, and it suits us. I can't afford to pay for a new factory. What'll become of us I don't know.'

His wife said nothing, and he sighed, stood up, stretched himself and began to carry the dishes over to the sink. But he scarcely knew what he was doing. As he had told his wife, he was worried.

Mr Harry Turnbull was the manager and owner of a gnome factory. The factory, as he called it, was nothing but a huge shed – or rather, three sheds knocked into one – in which half a dozen workmen manufactured garden ornaments. They made sundials, birdbaths, little statues of Cupid, and such-like things; but the Turnbull factory was especially noted for its garden gnomes. These were very popular among the people who had little gardens on the outskirts of the town. The gnomes were made of concrete and painted, red, green and brown. Some of them stood up with their legs apart and their arms akimbo; some were sitting cross-legged on concrete toadstools; some were made to squat at the edges of garden pools, fishing. Mr Turnbull also made plaster frogs and toads and giant snails. His business did pretty well, for his work was widely known amongst shopkeepers who sold garden tools and ornaments.

Every morning at eight o'clock Mr Turnbull would unlock the gate of his yard, and his workmen would come in and begin moulding and painting the ornaments. These were packed up and sent by road or rail all over the country. Mr Turnbull had to work hard to sell enough, for he kept his prices low. But he was proud of the business he had built up; and he would often smile with pleasure to see a row of newly painted gnomes of all sizes waiting to be sent away to his many customers.

Now Mr Turnbull did not own the land on which his factory and his house stood. It belonged to a rich landlord called Sir Midas Pike. So long as Harry Turnbull paid his rent regularly, Sir Midas left him alone. But it so happened that many of the old houses and buildings in the neighbourhood were being pulled down to make room for new shops and offices. Sir Midas began to see that the land he owned was worth a good deal more than his tenants paid him. He thought he would sell it to a big company which would pull down Mr Turnbull's three sheds and put up a huge new office building. While he was making up his mind whether to give Mr Turnbull notice to leave his factory, he decided to put up his rent. So he got his lawyer to send Mr Turnbull a very serious letter, typewritten on crisp blue note-paper, telling him he must pay double the rent he had been paying for the past twenty years. It was this which was worrying poor Harry Turnbull.

'Why can't everybody be content with the money they earn,'

he said to himself as he dried up the dishes, 'instead of trying to screw more out of poor people that can't afford it?'

But he knew it was no use talking like that. Sir Midas would have his rent, or the factory would be pulled down. Of that Mr Turnbull was certain.

'Cheer up, dear,' said his wife. 'We shall manage somehow. We always have so far.'

'Ah, it's all right for you to talk, Mabel,' he said, , 'but it's me who has to find the money for that thieving old landlord.'

'He's not a bad landlord,' said Mrs Turnbull. 'I've heard you say so yourself. Only he's like the rest of us – he doesn't want to miss the chance of making a bit more money. All the same, I own it would be a pity to leave this place. Perhaps we shan't be turned out after all.'

'Well, I hope not, my dear,' said Mr Turnbull, 'for I'm sure I don't know where we'd go.'

That was the worst of the trouble. Mr and Mrs Turnbull liked the neighbourhood, and they didn't welcome the idea of all the old houses and buildings they had known for twenty years being pulled down to make room for great blocks of offices. They knew the people of the neighbourhood, who liked and respected them.

Among the neighbours whom the Turnbulls were especially fond of were the children of the orphanage. This was a great grey building which stood next door to the gnome factory. It was old-fashioned and inclined to be cold in winter, but the ladies who managed it had done their best to make it comfortable for the twenty or thirty little boys and girls who lived there. The children had plain food and very plain clothes, but they were always happy, for everyone was kind to them, and they were allowed to make as much noise as they liked. Now the one thing which was lacking at the orphanage was a playground. There simply was not enough space for the children to run about in. On fine days they were taken to the park or the recreation ground and allowed to run among the trees and play on the seesaw and the swings. But the helpers at the orphanage did not always have time to take the children there, for the park was a long way off.

Mr Turnbull's gnome factory was separated from the orphanage by only a wooden fence, and the children used to climb over this and explore his factory yard. On fine evenings, after the men had gone home at five o'clock, they would scramble over the fence and chase each other among the packing-cases and piles of sand. Sometimes they would get into a shed used for storing bags of cement.

The helpers at the orphanage tried to stop the children from doing this, as they did not like them to trespass. But Mr Turnbull told them he didn't mind, so long as the children left the cement alone and were careful not to touch the freshly painted garden ornaments. They were better in the factory yard than in the streets, he said. Mr Turnbull, you see, was a kind man, and he liked the sound of the children playing near him. That was another reason why he didn't want to move to a new district.

Next morning the sun was shining, and Harry Turnbull had half-forgotten his worries when he stepped across the factory yard to unlock the gates. Then he opened the doors of the factory itself and inspected the rows of gnomes, the sundials and the birdbaths, with pride. The paint had dried on the green and red gnomes which had been finished yesterday, and today these would be packed up in wood shavings, inside boxwood crates, to be taken off to the railway station. There was plenty to do.

Turning round, he saw a shock-headed little boy standing in the doorway.

'May I come in, Mr Harry?' asked the boy.

'Sure enough, Tom,' said Mr Turnbull. 'Have you finished breakfast already?'

Tom came into the shed, followed by a bright-eyed little girl named Hannah and another girl who was so fair-haired that everyone called her the Angel. But she was the naughtiest of all the orphans.

The three children came in and began to look round. The Angel was already gazing delightedly at a little brown gnome sitting on a red mushroom.

'Come away, my dear,' said Harry. 'Don't you get too close, or there'll be an accident.'

Then two more boys came in. One of them was looking excited.

'What's the news, young Jacky?' asked Mr Turnbull.

'Please, mister, it's burglars again,' answered the boy. 'Little Sid here heard a policeman talking to Miss Larkins about it. They've been and burgled one of the big houses up on the hill.'

'They might come and take your little elves,' said the Angel.

'Burglars don't bother with stuff like this,' answered Mr Turnbull. 'It's jewels and money and silver and such-like stuff they're after – stuff they can carry away in their pockets.'

Then the foreman arrived, together with two of the workmen, and the day's work began. The children were cleared out into the yard, where they played happily in the sand. Mr Turnbull went back to the house to have breakfast.

Mrs Turnbull showed him the paper. There was a short report

about the activities of a gang of thieves led by one Joe Silence, so called because no one ever heard him come or go. They had broken into a bank at night in the centre of London and several big houses on the outskirts of the city. They had got away with money, jewels and fur coats, and police had been unable to find a trace of them. They worked in a silent, methodical way, taking what they wanted without breaking locks or windows, and never harming human beings. Sometimes they came while the owners were out at the theatre or a dinner party; sometimes they chose a week-end when the people were down by the sea. One night they would burgle a house on the far side of London; then nothing would be heard of them for a week or two. Next they would turn up in quite another district. All sorts of rumours went round, but nothing definite was learnt about Joe Silence and his gang. And now, it seemed, they had visited a big house in the neighbourhood of the factory only last night, and got away with all the silver plate and some jewellery worth £5,000. The house was not very close to the gnome factory, of course, for no rich people lived just there; but about two miles away there was a district known as the Hill, a suburb laid out with broad avenues and green open spaces. This was where the 'posh' people lived, as the orphan children called them. The houses were large and had big gardens and sometimes two or three garages. The children never went up there to play because it was too respectable; besides, some of the city gentlemen who lived there kept dogs, and you never knew whether you might be chased by a fierce Alsatian. They preferred to keep to the poorer quarters where you could have fun and people weren't so fussy.

Well, now there had been a burglary up on the Hill, and the police were going about making inquiries. Mr Turnbull had just finished his breakfast when there was a ring at the door.

'Perhaps it's the police,' said Mabel.

'What should they want with us?' asked Harry. 'Surely they know I'm not Mr Silence in disguise.'

'Well, let them in,' said his wife. 'I can't go like this, with my hands all covered in soapsuds.'

When Mr Turnbull opened the front door, he found a large

and very smart car drawn up outside. It was one of those long, glossy cars you see in advertisements. It was coloured cream and royal blue, and Mr Turnbull knew at once that it didn't belong to the police. A young man in chauffeur's uniform was standing stiffly at the front door.

'Are you Mr Turnbull, owner of the gnome factory?' asked the chauffeur. But before Harry could answer, he went on: 'Compliments of Sir Midas Pike, and would you be good enough to step over and speak to him?'

Harry's heart sank. Sir Midas Pike had called in person to see him! It could mean only one thing. He was to be turned out of his factory at once. He followed the chauffeur to the big car. Sir Midas had already alighted from it and was holding out his hand to greet his tenant. He was a fat man, very splendidly dressed, with a round, red face underneath his grey trilby hat. Harry had seen Sir Midas before, but he had never spoken to him. He was very nervous.

'If you've come about the rent, sir,' he began, but the fat man interrupted him.

'Rent?' he said. 'No, no, that can wait. Want to talk to you 'bout something else, if you can spare the time. Are you busy?'

'No, sir,' said Harry. 'Will you come into my office?'

He led the way round the side of the house and up some steps against one end of the factory. Sir Midas followed, puffing as he mounted the steps. He had a loud and pompous voice, but his manner was friendly. Fat men are usually friendly unless they lose their tempers. Harry wondered what on earth he wanted to talk about. He held open the door of the little upstairs room, and Sir Midas went in. The two men sat down on opposite sides of the desk.

Sir Midas Pike had a big red-brick house on the Hill. It had many gables and chimneys and wooden beams. There were three garages. A broad gravel drive swept up to the front door between rows of shrubs and flowering trees. The lawns were spacious and close-cropped. There were beds for all manner of flowers, a kitchen garden, and greenhouses for rare plants and early vegetables. The house was called 'Monte Carlo', and goodness knows how many servants were needed to run it! By far the most important person at 'Monte Carlo' was Sir Midas's wife, Bertha. Like her husband, she was stout, but she was also tall – much taller than Sir Midas, and this gave her a most imposing appearance. A few days ago she had been walking round the garden with her husband.

'What we need,' she said, 'is more ornaments. The garden looks bare. We've got a summer-house where nobody ever sits, and a swimming-pool where nobody ever swims. When you're up in the City and I've nothing to do but walk round the garden, I feel lonesome.'

'I could get a statue or two,' said Sir Midas. 'Something on horseback made of marble, perhaps, or a Roman god.'

'Not friendly,' said Lady Pike. 'Those heathen gods and goddesses remind me of a public park. Besides, they're chilly. No. I want something more friendly. Some little gnomes – that's what I'd like. Gnomes.'

'I see. What's an 'ome without a gnome, eh?'

Sir Midas roared with laughter at his own joke.

'Yes, they're homely. I strolled down the Avenue the other day, and I thought they looked so nice, all those little red and green gnomes in the front gardens.'

'Well, I don't want to be like the people in the Avenue,' said Sir Midas. 'Why, some of them haven't even got cars. I couldn't lower myself to copy *them*!'

'We needn't have just one small gnome,' said Bertha. 'We can have lots of them – big ones. I can see them now, all down the drive – fishing in the pool – squatting by the summer-house. Please, Midas, let there be gnomes.'

'I'll think about it,' said her husband.

And so a few days later, on his way to the office in the new royal blue and cream limousine, he called on Harry Turnbull at his factory, and told him what he wanted.

'Two dozen large-sized garden figures, painted in full colours,' said Harry. 'That's quite an order, Sir Midas.'

'Well, I'm sure you can manage it,' said Sir Midas in his loud, friendly voice, getting up from the desk. 'I'll pay whatever you ask. See that I get them by the end of the month.'

'The end of the month?' repeated Harry. 'I'll do my best, sir.'

' 'Course you will. Now I can't stay any longer. I'm late for the office as it is.'

And Sir Midas waddled down the steps and back to his car, where the chauffeur was standing stiffly by the open door. He got in, and the chauffeur got in, and immediately the car leapt smoothly forward with hardly a sound.

Mr Turnbull was speechless.

'What an order!' he thought. 'Two dozen outsize gnomes in full colours, ready and delivered by the end of the month. How on earth am I to manage it? Still, Sir Midas is my landlord. But he said nothing about the rent – that's something to be thankful for.'

Harry went inside the factory to talk over the matter with his foreman.

Soon all the workmen were busy making Sir Midas Pike's twenty-four gnomes. Two of them worked on the clay moulds, another mixed the cement for the finished figures, and Harry Turnbull went about seeing that their workmanship was of the best. The children from the orphanage ran in and out among the packing-cases and heaps of sand, and sometimes they peeped inside the big sheds to see what was going on.

'Look,' said Little Sid, who always liked to be first with the news, 'they're making sort of giant dwarfs. Wonder who they're for.'

Tom asked Mr Turnbull.

'They're for a very important gentleman who lives up on the Hill,' he was told.

In spite of all the effort that was put into the work, it did not go well. After a few days the foreman had an accident. He slipped on a patch of wet clay and broke the mould he was carrying, so that it had to be made again right from the start. What was worse, he sprained his ankle and had to stay at home for several days. Within a fortnight of the end of the month the work was hardly begun. One figure was finished and still wanted painting.

'We shall never do it in time,' said Harry to his wife. 'With such a run of bad luck as this, we shan't get half of them finished.'

Then one of the workmen got influenza and he too stayed at home; two more of them caught it from him, so that soon Harry was left with only two workmen – one of them no more than an apprentice – to carry out the whole order.

Harry was just thinking of going to see his landlord to explain his difficulties when Sir Midas himself telephoned the factory. His voice was so loud and clear that Harry had to hold the telephone half a yard away from his ear in order not to be deafened.

'Is that you, Mr Turnbull?' shouted Sir Midas. 'About those garden gnomes. How are you getting on with them? But I needn't ask. I'm sure you'll have done them in time.'

'Yes, sir,' Harry put in, 'but you see, sir –'

'Now look here,' went on Sir Midas, 'I tell you what. Me and my lady are going abroad on the first of next month – South of France, see, for a bit of sunshine. I want those gnomes delivered not later than the day before. That'll be the last day of this month, as agreed. I've promised Bertha and I don't want to disappoint her. I know I can depend on you. Good-bye.'

Before Harry could say anything in reply, Sir Midas had rung off.

Very sadly Harry went down into the yard. Little Sid and the Angel were see-sawing on a plank placed over an empty barrel. Jacky and Hannah were chasing each other back and forth across the yard. Tom was strolling about, doing nothing in particular.

'What's the matter, Mr Harry?' he asked, seeing his friend's unhappy expression. Harry told him.

'It's no good, Tom,' he said. 'I shall be turned out of this place for sure. Can't pay the rent, and if I don't deliver those gnomes on time, the landlord will kick me out. He won't have anything more to do with me.'

Tom told him everything would be all right. He was sure it would. But Harry was not to be consoled.

'It's all up with me, boy,' he said. 'We'll be lucky if we finish four of the blinking gnomes in time, let alone twenty-four. Wish I'd never promised to make the darned things.'

'Cheer up, Mr Harry,' said Tom. 'It won't be so bad as you think. You must go and talk to this landlord chap. I don't suppose he's bad at heart, not really.'

'Perhaps you're right,' agreed Harry. 'But he won't let me get a word in edgeways. Still, if I can get hold of him, I'll see what can be done.'

Next morning the worst blow of all fell. It was another long blue letter from Sir Midas Pike's lawyer. So far as Mr Turnbull could understand it, he was given three months' notice to leave the factory. The land was wanted, said the letter, 'for purposes of development', whatever that meant.

This was the end, thought Harry. If only he had been able to finish the twenty-four figures in time! Perhaps if they had pleased Sir Midas and Lady Pike, Sir Midas would have let him keep the factory. But of course there wasn't a chance that the gnomes would be finished. Lady Pike would be angry, and her husband would be furious, and would certainly not listen to poor Harry. Harry was so miserable that he felt like telling the workmen to break up the figures they had finished and go off and get themselves other jobs. What was the use of going on? He sat at the kitchen table with the letter in his hand, unable to touch his breakfast.

When the last day of the month came, five of the figures had been finished. The foreman had returned; although he still limped badly with his sprained ankle, he was able to carry on with his work. The three others had got over their flu and had come back. But it was too late to do much good. However, it was decided to pack up the five finished gnomes on to a lorry and take them up to 'Monte Carlo' in the afternoon. Perhaps Sir Midas would be pleased with them even though the whole two dozen were not ready. They looked very smart in their fresh green and red paint. One was standing with his hands on his hips, laughing mischievously. Another was squatting cross-legged on the ground. The third was seated on a scarlet toadstool, the fourth was standing with his legs astride on a concrete tortoise, and the fifth had a fishing-rod in his hand with which to fish in the swimming-pool. If only they had managed to finish another seven, making up the first dozen! That would have been something. As it was, the five gnomes, smart and lively as they were, looked a pathetically small band.

Harry went to the telephone to arrange with a carrier to bring his lorry in the afternoon, for the factory-owner had no lorry of his own.

Meanwhile, nothing more had been heard in the neighbourhood about Joe Silence and his gang of thieves. But this very day they were planning another visit to the Hill. They had done very well there the time before, and the police had altogether failed to get on their track. They had planned to make a raid on the home of Sir Midas Pike, whose wife was known to have a hoard of expensive jewellery as well as at least two superb fur coats. While Joe and his men were planning the robbery, they discovered that Sir Midas and his wife were going abroad on the first day of the following month. No doubt the furs and jewels would go with them. So Joe arranged a daring attempt for the very night before their departure. Usually he liked to be quite certain a house was empty before paying it a visit, but this time he decided to take the risk. He found out through a friend of his, who happened to know one of the servants at 'Monte Carlo', that Sir Midas and Lady Pike were going out to dinner and would not be back till late. In some ways this was an ideal op-portunity. For when the master and mistress were out, the ser-vants usually had the evening off; and there would probably be a good deal of cash, jewellery and other valuables lying about waiting to be packed up for the journey next day.

That was why Joe Silence picked on the last night of the month to pay a call at the big house on the Hill.

But Joe and his friends were not the only ones making plans that day. After the midday meal at the orphanage, Tom called together his particular friends and told them he wanted to have a meeting. They didn't gather in the yard of the gnome factory this time, but in a dark, musty shed behind the coal-hole at the orphan-age. This shed was used for nothing in particular, and the children always went there for any special private meetings.

'It's about Harry,' said Tom. 'We've got to help him, see.'

'What's wrong?' asked another boy.

'It's all because of the gnomes what he couldn't get done in time,' explained Little Sid.

'He's going to be turned out of his factory if he doesn't finish them,' said Jacky. 'Then we'll have nowhere to play.'

'Is it true they're going to pull down the factory and put up a petrol station?' asked Hannah.

'That'd be smashing,' said the Angel. 'I love cars.'

'Silly!' retorted Tom. 'They don't allow kids to play round petrol stations. If Harry's landlord turns him out, I tell you, we shan't have any playground.'

'Well, what can we do?'

'We can't go and stick a knife in the landlord.'

'No, but we might go and see him. We could explain.'

'He wouldn't listen to *us*. He's a big fat man with two cars. He must be very rich to order twenty-four giant dwarfs.'

So the council went on. Nobody could think of an easy way of helping Harry out of his trouble. But the children were not discouraged.

The lorry had been promised for half-past three. But Mr Turnbull's bad luck was not yet at an end. At a quarter-past, the carrier telephoned to say that the lorry had broken down. Something had gone wrong with the gear-box. No, he was sorry, he hadn't another lorry to spare that day. Harry told him he must get it put right and come as soon as he could. It was very important that the load should be moved that day. The carrier said he would do the best he could. He had a man working on the gear-box at that very moment. There was nothing for it but to wait. Mrs Turnbull made everyone a cup of tea, and they all settled down to fill in time till the lorry came.

It was not till six o'clock that they heard the sound of brakes outside the factory yard. The lorry pulled up at the gates, and immediately Harry and the foreman began to load it with the five garden gnomes. They packed the figures very carefully with straw, so as to make sure they would not get damaged if the lorry had to pull up suddenly. The other workmen had been sent home, since Harry and the foreman could do all the necessary work themselves. They were so busy that they did not notice two or three of the orphans from next door darting hither and thither, watching all that went on. At last the lorry was ready to go. The foreman went behind to look after the figures, and Harry got up beside the driver. Just as they were going to start, Tom ran up and asked Harry if he might come with him. He often went with the factory-owner when he was delivering goods by road.

'I think we can find room,' said Mr Turnbull.

The carrier made no objection, and Tom hopped up beside the two men in the driver's cabin.

At last the carrier started up the engine, and they drove off.

'Well,' thought Harry. 'It's the best we can do. At least we'll deliver *some* of the stuff before the end of the month – that is, if we don't have another smash.'

But they drove up the hill and reached 'Monte Carlo' without mishap. The journey was only two miles, but they went slowly so as not to damage the cargo; and it was after six-thirty when they got to the house.

The carrier steered the lorry carefully up the long gravel drive and stopped near the side door. Harry got out and rang the bell. A little squint-eyed man-servant asked him what he wanted.

'I'd like to speak to Sir Midas Pike. It's rather important.'

'Well, you can't. He's out. Been gone these ten minutes. What do you want?'

Harry told him he had come to deliver the five gnomes.

The squint-eyed man hesitated. He knew that Joe Silence was coming this evening. The other servants had already gone out, and except for himself the house was empty. Even the Alsatian dog was asleep in his kennel at the other side of the building. The man-servant didn't want strangers hanging about, but it wouldn't do to make them suspicious.

'You'd better unload the stuff and leave it. I'll tell the master you came. He won't be back till late. I suppose he knows what it is?'

'Oh yes,' said Harry. 'He's expecting it.'

'All right,' said the servant. 'Be quick about it.'

He shut the door in Harry's face and left him to unload the lorry.

It did not take them long to lift down the five figures and place them carefully along either side of the drive. They placed two on each side, and the fifth – the one with the fishing-rod – they carried to the swimming-pool and set it up overlooking the water.

'There,' said Harry. 'Now old Pike and his lady will be sure to see them when they come home. There's a full moon tonight, and if the sky's clear, these little chaps won't look half bad. Let's hope her ladyship takes a fancy to them. They're the best I can do. Perhaps we can finish the other nineteen while they're away on holiday.'

Once more the three men and the boy climbed back into the lorry and drove away, leaving 'Monte Carlo' in the care of the squint-eyed servant and the five gnomes. As soon as they were back in the factory, Tom thanked Harry for the ride and ran off to find his companions. Harry went indoors to wash his hands and face and see what Mabel had got for supper.

That night 'Monte Carlo' and the neighbouring houses on the Hill lay calm and silent in the moonlight. A faint breeze rustled the tops of the flowering trees, beneath which the five gnomes stood motionless, as if awaiting the return of their new owners. Then suddenly, without warning, a strange thing happened. The garden became alive with gnomes. One moment it was still and deserted. The next moment it was full of darting figures. Occasionally these new gnomes breathed a hurried word to each other, and one of them seemed to be directing the rest.

'Over there!' it whispered, pushing a smaller gnome towards the edge of a flowerbed. Within a minute all the running figures had taken up positions in the garden, some crouching at the end of the drive, others posed beneath the trees, one squatting on a stone sundial in the centre of a rose-bed.

Together with the five gnomes already in position, there must have been quite two dozen in all. Not a sound came from them. They scarcely moved a muscle. Anyone seeing them at that moment would have thought they had been turned to stone.

Then something else happened, equally silent and unusual. A long black car pulled up noiselessly just outside the gates of 'Monte Carlo', and three men got out. They were dressed in dark clothes and had masks over the upper halves of their faces. They left the doors of the car open and crept up the drive. They moved swiftly, treading on the grass instead of the gravel in order to avoid making a noise. One of them almost knocked over a cement figure which stood with its arms akimbo on the edge of the grass. The man muttered a curse and went on.

'Quiet, you!' whispered one of the other men.

'Okay, Joe,' answered the one who had tripped over the gnome.

When they reached the front door of the house, the man who had been addressed as 'Joe' pushed the door open, and they all went inside.

Back at the orphanage Miss Larkins, who had been sitting up late working at her accounts, got up to make herself a cup of tea before going to bed. On her way past the biggest of the four bedrooms where the children slept, she paused for a moment to listen. Not a sound came from the room. All was well. Then something made her open the door quietly and look inside. Perhaps it was that the room was unusually silent. As a rule she could hear, even when the door was shut, an occasional sound of breathing, a cough, or some little boy murmuring in his sleep. What Miss Larkins saw in the moonlight streaming through the windows made her gasp with amazement. For what she saw was ten empty beds!

Miss Larkins quickly went round the other bedrooms and found that nine more children were missing. Only the very youngest orphans were sleeping peacefully. Nineteen of her charges had disappeared.

'The little monkeys!' she said to herself calmly.

Miss Larkins was not the person to worry until she was sure there was something to worry about.

Then she noticed something else unusual. At the end of one of the passages was a big old-fashioned cupboard in which were kept all sorts of clothes for dressing-up. The children loved charades and plays. The dressing-up cupboard was a favourite place on long winter evenings and wet days. Miss Larkins noticed that the door had been left open, and that the inside of the cupboard was distinctly untidy. Last Christmas there had been a play about dwarfs. Twenty of the boys and girls had dressed up in little green or brown costumes with pointed red caps. And now these costumes were missing. Miss Larkins knew they had gone, for she herself had folded them up neatly and piled them in a big cardboard box. The box was empty – except for one single costume.

'So,' she said to herself, 'nineteen little dwarfs have gone on a moonlight adventure. Where *can* they have got to?'

She went quickly next door and rang the bell of Mr Turnbull's house. She often called on her kind neighbours when there was any trouble at the orphanage. Not that she was worried, but she felt she ought to know where the children were. If she was going out looking for them in the middle of the night, she would need some help.

She explained everything quite calmly to Mr Turnbull, who thought it would be just as well to have a policeman with them. After all, when nineteen small children are playing gnomes in the middle of the night, and those children are supposed to be in your charge, you can't be too careful.

The police station was not far down the road. Sergeant Piper was almost due to go off duty when the telephone bell rang, and he heard the voice of his good friend, Harry Turnbull. Harry told him how matters stood. A few minutes later Sergeant Piper, Mr Turnbull and Miss Larkins were exploring the moonlit streets in a police car.

It had been the Angel's idea to borrow the costumes, dress up as gnomes, steal out of the orphanage after bed-time, and make their way up to Sir Midas Pike's house on the Hill. On his visit to the house earlier in the evening Tom had heard enough to know that Sir Midas and his wife would be coming home late that night and would expect to see twenty-four garden gnomes. But only five of the figures had actually been delivered. Very well – there would be nineteen *live* gnomes to greet them. Later, when Sir Midas and his lady were safely indoors, they could creep back home again and go to bed as if nothing had happened. Next day Harry could walk up to the big house and explain everything. Then perhaps Sir Midas would forgive him, and his troubles would be over. The Angel thought this was the most wonderful piece of mischief she had ever planned. To Tom and some of the others it seemed crazy. Still, it was the only way they could do anything to help Harry. It was a mild night, and the moon was full. Whatever happened, it would be a splendid lark, and nobody could be cross with them, for it was all done out of kindness.

Well, as you have heard, the children reached 'Monte Carlo' without any trouble and took up their positions in the garden to wait for the return of Sir Midas and Lady Pike. You can guess their amazement when the three silent men with masked faces crept up the drive and entered the house.

As soon as the door had closed behind the men, the live gnomes ran to their leader and gathered round him.

'I tell you what,' said Tom in a loud whisper. 'They're burglars – that's what they are.'

'Oh, I'm scared!' said the Angel.

'So am I,' agreed Hannah.

'Never mind that,' said Jacky. 'We've got to stop them.'

'There's only three of 'em,' put in Little Sid. 'We can tackle them between us.'

'Look here, kids,' said Tom, 'listen carefully and do as I tell you.'

Like a born general he swiftly told his followers exactly what each was to do when the thieves came out of the house. In a very few minutes all the nineteen children were back in their places. It would not do for the burglars to notice anything wrong at first. The children were not a moment too soon, for Joe Silence and his two companions had also been working swiftly inside the house. The squint-eyed man-servant had gone to bed. He had better not know anything about the burglary. When the men came out of the front door, the leader, Joe Silence, was carrying a little black bag full of silver and jewellery; the second had two soft, luxurious fur coats over his arm, and the third had his pockets bulging with foreign bank-notes and other valuables.

As soon as they were clear of the front door and had begun to creep down the drive towards their car, the shrill voice of the chief gnome rang out loud and clear in the moonlit garden.

'Thieves!' he shouted. 'Stop thieves! Quick, kids – you know what to do!'

He ran at the leader and grabbed the black bag, racing across the garden with it to throw it into the bushes. Joe cursed and ran after him. Two other gnomes seized the fur coats from the second thief before he could recover from his surprise; another two tripped up the third, who crashed down on to the gravel drive. Then a wild chase began. A dozen gnomes tore round the garden screaming 'Thieves, thieves!' at the top of their voices. The man who had had the black bag was trying to get it back. He dodged here and there over the flowerbeds and between the shrubs, but the children were too nimble for him. One of them led the thief to the edge of the pool, then jumped to one side, and Joe lost his footing and went headlong into the water. The shouts of the children woke the Alsatian, who was dozing in the backyard. He could not get loose from his chain, but he started up a barking which set all the other dogs on the Hill in an uproar. Dogs are always restless at full moon, and the frenzied baying at 'Monte Carlo' sent them all mad at once. Never had there been such a barking and yapping in the respectable neighbourhood of the Hill.

'Quick, men!' ordered Joe Silence, as he climbed out of the pool in his dripping clothes. 'Let's beat it! The car – get the car started!'

But he was too late. Half a dozen children had been detailed by Tom to put the car out of action. They had dragged the cement garden gnomes down the drive and wedged one of them in front of each of the wheels. The fifth gnome had been shoved inside between the driving-seat and the gear lever. Anyone who wanted to start the car would first have to get rid of this obstacle. By the time the thieves had decided to make their escape, the car-busters were amusing themselves by smashing the windows with stones from Sir Midas's rockery. As a result of this glorious attack, the inside of the car was by now strewn with broken glass. The thieves were too intent on getting away to spare much time for their enemies; but when one of the men made an angry dart at the children, they leapt out of reach, screaming 'Thieves! Robbers! Murderers!'

The barking of the dogs had roused the neighbours, and those who had not yet gone to bed ran to the house to see what was going on. Others came out in dressing-gowns, and several passing cars had stopped so that their owners could find out the cause of the extraordinary disturbance. Then the scream of a police siren was heard above the commotion. Sergeant Piper directed his car at high speed towards the gates, scattering the onlookers in all directions. It pulled up bumper to bumper with the thieves' car, head on. The sergeant, Miss Larkins and Mr Turnbull jumped out.

After a brief chase among the bushes, the policeman, Harry, and three of the bystanders had little difficulty in arresting the burglars. In the police car was a radio, and in a very few minutes the sergeant had called up two more policemen to help him escort Joe Silence and his companions to the station.

Miss Larkins gathered her orphans around her, and had very soon made sure that all nineteen of them were present. Apart from torn clothes and an assortment of cuts and bruises they were none the worse for their daring adventure.

Sir Midas's servants had by now all returned, and were considerably surprised to see what had been going on. But no one was more surprised than the master and mistress of the house, who presently returned in their royal blue and cream limousine.

There was a great deal of explaining to be done.

'I think,' said Sir Midas to the sergeant, 'you had better arrest this fellow too.'

He pointed to the squint-eyed servant, who was now standing at the front door in his dressing-gown, pretending he had only just woken up.

When the police had gone off with the thieves, the neighbours went home, and calm was restored on the Hill. Even the dogs stopped barking and settled down to sleep. Then Sir Midas invited Harry, Miss Larkins and all the children into the house to be given refreshments. He thanked them for saving his property and congratulated them on bringing the notorious Joe Silence to justice. The beds and bushes in the garden had been searched, as well as the pockets of the thieves, and all the stolen property was found. Sir Midas and Lady Pike were delighted. They promised to consider the matter of a suitable reward. It was not till nearly dawn that the nineteen weary gnomes were driven home in three car-loads, to curl up happily in the empty beds at the orphanage.

But that wasn't quite the end. In a way, it was only the beginning. For – to cut short a very long tale – Harry Turnbull and his wife were allowed to rent a new and better factory in the same neighbourhood, paying no more for it than they had paid for the old one. As for the old factory, Sir Midas had a splendid idea – or rather, it was really Bertha's idea. Although she was so commanding, she was a kind woman, and was determined to do something for the orphanage. As a reward for the capture of the thieves, the old gnome factory was pulled down, and the yard was cleared to make room for a fine new playground. It was planted with grass; and a roundabout, several swings and a slide were put up for the children to play on. The Turnbulls' house was not pulled down, but was given to Miss Larkins and her assistants, so as to make room for even more children in the orphanage.

The five garden gnomes had been rescued from under the thieves' car, and were found to be hardly damaged at all. They were soon patched up and given a new coat of paint. Once more they were set up in the garden at 'Monte Carlo'. Lady Pike said that five were really quite enough, so Sir Midas cancelled the order for the other nineteen. This didn't bother Harry in the least, for he had plenty of work to do, and he had never liked making such unusually large figures. Lady Pike joined the committee of the orphanage, and often invited the children to visit her on the Hill. This made her feel less lonely, and she was glad to think she was doing something useful.

So began a time of new and greater happiness for everyone – for Sir Midas and Bertha at 'Monte Carlo', for Miss Larkins and the orphans, and for Mr and Mrs Turnbull at the new gnome factory.

The Witch's Castle

The wood was dark and thick. It was not safe to go there towards nightfall, for evil things happened. In the middle of the wood was an ancient, stern castle, grey and frowning. In it lived a witch, an old woman with hard, wicked eyes, a wrinkled skin, and hands like claws. All who saw her were afraid. Even the animals shrank from her. But few saw her in daylight, for every morning she would turn herself into an owl or a cat – a lean and cruel cat with green eyes and sharp claws. She would roam through the forest catching little creatures to kill and cook for supper in the evening, when she turned herself back into a witch.

The witch had enchanted the ground about her castle, so that if anyone came within a hundred steps of it they were made to stand quite still until she gave them leave to move once more. The only creatures she allowed within this magic circle were young girls. If any came into the circle she turned them into birds and fastened them up in cages of basketwork. These she kept in a cold, dark room in the castle, never allowing them to see the light of day. She had more than a thousand of these cages, each with its sad little wood-pigeon, canary or nightingale.

One sunny day in spring two people walked in the forest, not far from the witch's castle. One was a sweet girl named Rosamund, as young and beautiful a maiden as had ever lived in that country. Her friend was a young man called Godfrey. He was tall, straight and handsome. They were happy, for Godfrey had asked Rosamund to marry him, and this she had promised to do if her parents agreed. Neither had any doubt that their parents would be pleased, for hers were fond of Godfrey, and Godfrey's parents loved Rosamund. For hours the two lovers walked in the wood, and forgot about the passing of time. Before long the sun had almost gone down behind the trees.

'We must go home,' Godfrey said. 'It is late, and we must not get lost, or we may wander near the witch's castle.'

At this Rosamund shuddered, for everyone knew of the witch and her evil ways.

But sad to tell, the two young people lost their path, and as evening fell they sat down for a while under a tree, because Rosamund was weary. Above her in the branches she heard a wood-pigeon crooning sadly to itself.

Rosamund too began to sing softly, and as Godfrey listened, he also became sad. It seemed as if all their happiness was over. All at once he turned and looked through the trees and, as he did so, he became cold with fear. There, for the first time, he noticed the frowning walls of the witch's castle, and knew that danger was near. He was about to seize Rosamund by the hand and escape with her from the danger, when the little song she was singing suddenly turned into the notes of a nightingale. He was too late. Rosamund was not there. Instead, upon a branch of the tree under which she had been singing, sat a little brown bird, and a great screech-owl was circling round it, crying 'Tu-whit, tu-whit, tu-whoo!' Rosamund had been changed into a nightingale.

At the same moment Godfrey too fell under the witch's spell. He found himself unable to move. He could not even call out the name of Rosamund. The screech-owl vanished into the thicket just as the sun faded behind the trees. Almost immediately a hideous old woman appeared and beckoned to the nightingale to come down from its branch. The witch had a basketwork cage in her hand. Into this she put the nightingale, clapping the cage-door shut. The bird was her prisoner. She took it away and placed the cage in the cold, dark room in the castle, Then she returned to where Godfrey stood, still helpless, as if rooted to the place where he had last seen Rosamund.

The witch spoke to him in her cruel, hard voice, telling him he

might go on condition that he left the castle as fast as possible and never came near it again.

At last Godfrey found his voice. 'Give me back the maiden I love,' he begged. 'At least let me see Rosamund and speak to her once more.'

'You shall never see her again, young man. Now go – and remember, get away from here as far as you can, or you will be turned to stone.'

Godfrey had nothing to do but to obey. Stumbling through the darkness, he made off as fast as he could, determined to begin his search for Rosamund on the morrow.

For many days he looked for someone who might help him in his search, but all were terrified at the very thought of the witch and her enchantments. For weeks he strayed here and there, until one night he sank down to sleep at the edge of a meadow, overcome with weariness and despair. His sleep was restless and troubled. Towards morning he had a dream. He dreamed that he saw growing on a hillside a single blood-red flower with a great pearl in its centre. He stooped and picked the flower and went away with it. Then his dream faded, and he awoke. Somehow he knew that he must find this flower, for it alone could help him to recover the maiden he loved.

So for many days Godfrey went about the countryside, asking everyone he met if they had seen a blood-red flower, growing by

itself. No one could help him, and many thought the young man was mad.

Then one day, just as he was beginning to lose hope, the morning sun revealed to him, on a far hillside, something that glowed and sparkled in the grass. He ran towards it, and when he was near enough to see it clearly, he knew that it was what he was looking for – a single blood-red flower with a great drop of dew in the centre, sparkling like a pearl in the sunlight.

The young man picked the flower with trembling hands. Then began the long journey back to the castle. For days he travelled over field and moor, across rivers, through forests, never losing the flower which he believed would bring him happiness.

When he was a hundred steps from the castle, Godfrey was delighted to find that the witch's spells had no power over him. He moved as easily within the magic circle as outside it. He strode up to the great doorway and touched it with the flower. Instantly it flew open. In the courtyard he stood and listened for the singing of birds. He entered an inner door and began to explore the cold and dismal corridors of the castle. At last he heard the sound he had been listening for – the chirping and singing of hundreds of birds. The sound led him to the dark room where the old woman kept her cages. As he entered the room, she was feeding the birds, pushing scraps of crust and seeds between the bars for her hungry prisoners.

At first the witch did not hear Godfrey approach because of

the noise of the birds. When she saw him she was seized with
anger. She cursed and stormed at the young man, but she had no
power over him. She sprang at him with her bony claws, but she
could not come within two steps of him. The flower he held had
power to break all her enchantments.

The next thing to be done was to find the cage containing his
beloved nightingale. He searched high and low, but there were
hundreds of nightingales. All at once, Godfrey saw the old woman
craftily creeping away with a cage in her hand. Something told
him that this must be the cage he had been seeking. Just as the
witch reached the door, Godfrey leaped towards her and touched
both the old woman and the cage with the scarlet flower. Instantly

she lost her power of enchantment. She screamed horribly, and cursed the young man, but he took no notice, and the witch ran from the room and was seen no more.

At the touch of the flower, the basketwork cage had sprung open and the nightingale was free. With a glad burst of song it was turned instantly into the fair maiden whom Godfrey had sought so long. It was his own Rosamund. As she clung to him, her arms fast round his neck, they saw that all the other cages had opened and the birds flown out. They too were turned into young and lovely maidens, so that all the witch's evil was undone.

The young man and his betrothed lost no time in getting as far away from the frowning castle as possible. When they returned home, their parents were overjoyed to see them, and preparations were made for the marriage. Rosamund and Godfrey lived happily for the rest of their long lives, and never feared the enchanted castle again.

The Stonemason
of Elphinstone

This is a story about the village of Elphinstone, and how it got its
name. The village is not the one in Scotland, but another of the
same name in one of the northern counties of England. In the
centre of the village stands a church, with a great stone tower. If
you look up at the top of the tower, you will see that at each
corner is a gargoyle – that is, a strange figure carved in stone
leaning out so that the rain which falls on the roof of the tower
may trickle out of the creature's mouth on to the ground below.
The four gargoyles at the top of Elphinstone tower are all different, and one of them is very strange indeed. But let us start
the story at the beginning, which is the proper place to start,
after all.

Many years ago – it might have been five hundred and it might
have been more – there was a knight living in the north country
called Sir John Tilbury. Now he was getting old, and he had made
a great deal of money by the sale of wool, and he thought he
would like to do something with his money so that people would
remember him after he died. He decided to build a church. On
the edge of his land there were many poor people living, and they
had no church to go to nearer than ten miles. It would be a good
thing, thought Sir John, if they had a church of their own; so he
had plans made, and hired workmen – carpenters, labourers and
masons. The work went well, and before many years passed, the
church was nearly finished. It was a fine, tall building of grey
stone with richly carved window-frames and a great square tower
at the western end. The carpenters had put in the roof-timbers
and the glaziers had even put some of the glass into the

windows. Before long only a few finishing touches remained to be done.

Now one of the stonemasons at work on the church was a man named Martin. He was getting on for middle age, not very tall and with curly brown hair; his work in the open air had made his skin brown and weather-beaten, and his clothes and his hair and the wrinkles on his face were all filled with the dust of his trade. He was a good mason; there was no one better in all the country for squaring and trimming the grey stone blocks and smoothing the surface of them with his iron chisels. What he loved doing above everything else was carving stone figures, and oak leaves and vine leaves, and twisted patterns in stone to go round the arches of doors and windows. He had spent his life carving such things, and nobody could do it better than he.

But he had a fault. Few of us are perfect, and Martin was not what we should call a regular workman. Sometimes he would leave his work for a whole day, or even longer, and stay at home, or go wandering on the moors; he would even throw up a job altogether, when it was only half-done; or he would toss his mallet and his chisels into a leather bag and make off to the town to sit gossiping with travellers at an inn or a fairground. Time and again the master mason in charge of the work on the church would speak to Martin about his bad ways, sometimes he would even complain to Sir John himself, and Sir John would ask the master mason why he did not get rid of Martin and find somebody more reliable.

'Well, to tell you the truth, Sir John,' the master mason said, 'I can't find another like him for squaring a corner-stone or knocking a saint's head or a bunch of grapes or the devil himself – begging your pardon, Sir John! – out of a lump of stone. So I'm loath to get rid of him, you see. But if your lordship would have a word with him one day, perhaps he'd listen to you. It does seem a pity, sir, that it does, that a mason like him should be such an awkward, unserviceable fellow.'

Sir John said he would have a word with Martin next time he saw him at work.

Martin was a widower. His wife had died leaving him one son

and one daughter. Together they lived in a little cottage not far from where the church was being built. The boy worked for the blacksmith, and a very regular, trustworthy boy he was – not at all like his father, the people said. The daughter, Alison, was a good-looking, cheerful girl of sixteen years or so, and it was she who kept house for her father and her brother. She made their little cottage as neat and clean as a choir-boy on Sunday; she fed the hens, milked the cow, mended the clothes, cooked, washed, and did everything as if she had been a wife and mother herself. Sometimes she had to scold her father for coming in late for supper, or for staying out all night on the moors with his dog, but she loved him dearly and would not have made him unhappy for anything in the world.

Well, one evening Martin came home with a face as long and solemn as a sermon. He found Alison getting the supper ready.

'It's all up with me now,' said he. 'We're ruined, my dear, and no mistake.'

'Whatever's happened, father?' asked his daughter. 'Have you been dismissed from your work or what?'

'Not yet. But I shall be soon enough. It's no good, my love; I can't stick at a job and that's all there is about it. Never could. I'm so behindhand with my work that Sir John spoke to me about it himself today.'

'Sir John Tilbury?'

'Yes, Sir John himself, that's paying for the new church with the gold he got from selling wool to the Flemings across the sea. Over the moor he came on his white horse, with his old white beard fluttering in the wind like a pinafore on a clothes-line. I could have carved him out of stone for Herod the Great or King Alfred himself, so noble and fine he looked. Straight up to me he comes, just where I stood, chipping away at Saint Peter with his shepherd's crook that's to go over the door to the south porch when I get him finished.'

'And what did he say?' asked Alison impatiently.

'Well, to cut a long story short, my dear,' answered her father, 'he said I was working too slow and I must finish by Hallowe'en or he'd push me out.'

'Hallowe'en!' said Alison. 'Why, that's not for another six weeks. How much is there left to do?'

'Let's see,' said Martin. 'When I've finished Saint Peter with his shepherd's crook, there's the battlements round the top of the tower and the four gargoyles at the four corners. I think that's about all.'

'That's not so bad,' said Alison. 'Just you get to bed early, go to work as soon as it's light, and don't go gadding off to the town, and you'll finish it in good time.'

'It's easy enough for you to say that!' exclaimed Martin. 'Carving stone isn't like making pastry-pies, my girl. There's a tidy lot left to do. Unless the fairies, or Merlin the wizard, or Old Nick himself gives me a hand, I don't know how I shall get it done, and that's the truth.'

'For shame, father!' said Alison. 'That's no way to talk. Now just you shake that dust from your clothes and wash your face and hands and by that time supper will be ready. It's something you like, too, so don't be long. I can't make pies the same as you carve saints, I know, but I don't waste so much time about it. Cheer up, now, there's a good father.'

Presently the boy came in, and they all sat down to supper. Early to bed went Martin, determined to make an early start at the church.

At first things went fairly well. Martin went regularly to work, and for hours he would do nothing but chip away at the blocks of stone, scraping and smoothing; then he would climb the wooden scaffolding to the top of the tower and fix the blocks in position. The master mason was pleased with his progress, and pleased too that he had thought of asking Sir John to have a word with Martin. On wet days, when it was impossible to work outside, Martin would sit inside the almost finished church carving away at one of the four gargoyles that were to be placed at the corners of the tower. It was in the form of a long-necked dog with fierce eyes and jaws wide open to let the water pour through. With great care Martin carved the two rows of sharp teeth and the curved, pointed tongue. What a fine carver he was, thought the master mason, and what a good thing it was that he was working so steadily.

Then, when the stone dog was finished, and there were still three weeks left before Hallowe'en – which, you remember, was the date set for finishing the work – Martin felt it was time he had a day off. So calling to his dog to follow, he strode away over the moors to the town. There he fell in with some companions, and together they spent the day chatting and laughing and telling stories.

It was late when he got home that evening, and next day he again did not feel like work.

'What's a man for,' he asked himself, 'if he has to work every blessed moment of the day scratching and scraping at lumps of stone?'

So once more he set off with his dog, this time to a fair some miles distant, where there were jugglers and wrestlers to be seen, and ballad-singers to hear.

That evening when he got home, his daughter scolded him.

'That's the second day you've not been to the church, father,' she said. 'What's to become of us when you are thrown out of work, I should like to know?'

'I'll not be thrown out of work,' said Martin. 'The job's nearly finished, I tell you, and there's near three weeks left. Why, I could finish it in time if I had but one hand!'

'Well, get your supper now,' she said, 'and off to bed with you, for you must start early in the morning if you're to make up for lost time.'

'Lost time!' repeated her father scornfully. 'If a man can't take time off once in a way, he might as well be a Hebrew slave working for Pharaoh of Egypt. Besides, the job's nearly finished, I tell you!'

But it was not nearly finished, and he knew it. The battlements round the tower were only half-done, and there were three more gargoyles to be carved and set in place.

Now one of Martin's favourite sports was poaching. He did not often do it, but sometimes when the night was fine and not too cold, and there was a moon shining, the wish to go wandering out of doors came strong upon him. It was forbidden to catch hares and rabbits and birds on Sir John Tilbury's land, but most of the men in the village went out now and again and caught a rabbit for the pot, and no one thought much harm of it.

One of the favourite haunts of poachers was a place called Ferry Hill, which belonged to Sir John. Now the name means 'Fairy Hill', for it is covered with trees and in the centre of the trees is a great mound, under which the country people in those days believed the fairies lived.

Well, one night, when his son and daughter were safely asleep, Martin took a thick stick and a sack and set off for Ferry Hill to see what luck he might have. The moon was full, and although there was a touch of frost in the air, it was not too cold for a night's sport.

Over the fields he went and up the hill. The moon, shining through the trees, made ghostly shadows, but nothing stirred. Not even an owl was abroad, and there was no sound except the

93

cracking of twigs and the rustle of fallen leaves under Martin's feet.

For a time he sat down on his sack and waited. Then he began to think of the work that he still had to do at the church, and he pictured the face of Sir John when he found that it was not finished in time. What would Sir John think, Martin wondered, if he knew that one of his stonemasons was even now trespassing on his land in the hope of catching a rabbit?

'Not much stirring tonight,' he said to himself. 'I'll just go up to the top of the hill; then if I see nothing, I'll be off home.'

So he got up, threw the sack over his shoulder, and made for the green mound in the centre of the wood.

Suddenly he stopped.

'Hello!' he said. 'Now what's that? Rabbit holes, I do believe.'

There, just below a grassy bank with brambles growing over it, were two or three round openings, like the entrances to little caves.

Martin bent down. It seemed as if he could hear movements inside the rabbit hole. Quickly he opened his sack and put the mouth of it over the largest hole.

'Now,' said the mason, 'may Saint Martin, who is my very own patron saint, send him out of his hole and into my sack!'

Even as he spoke, there was a scuffling sound inside the hole and something ran out of it right into the open sack. It kicked and struggled, but Martin, without waiting to look inside, closed the mouth of the sack and tied it into a knot. Then he threw it over his shoulder, picked up his cudgel and made off down the hill.

'A rabbit, I'll be bound,' said Martin. 'A nice fat rabbit, by the feel of him. And there's nobody can make a rabbit stew like my Alison!'

It was not long before he was back at his own cottage door.

Softly he lifted the latch and went in. There was not a sound to be heard. Son and daughter must be fast asleep. He put the sack on the floor and sat down on the bench beside the table. Without stopping to light a candle, for the full moon sent its light streaming through the window so that it was almost as bright as day, Martin untied the neck of the sack. But first he looked round to see that the door was shut, so that the rabbit could not escape.

Instantly there was a scurrying of limbs inside the sack and out ran – *not* a furry grey rabbit, but a two-legged creature dressed in brown, with the face of an old man! His little black eyes glittered in the moonlight. He wore a pointed cap of brown leather, and he stood about as high as the length of your fore-arm from the wrist to the elbow. He sprang first on the table and stood with his hands on his hips.

Martin had nearly shouted out in surprise at seeing the little man, but he managed to keep quiet for fear of waking his son and daughter. When he had recovered from his surprise, he said politely:

'Good evening to you. Who are you and what's your name?'

The little man answered him in rhyme.

> 'Who am I and what's my name?
> No man on earth can tell this same.
> If ever my name on earth is known,
> This same elf shall turn to stone.'

'That wouldn't do at all,' said Martin. 'But truth to say, I mistook you for a rabbit. I've no wish to go catching elves and fairies and such as you. I'll give you a shilling for your trouble, and you can be off home.'

'A shilling!' said the elf scornfully. 'Never offer me and my likes money! But if you'll give me some white bread and a bowl of milk, perhaps I can help you.'

'I'll give you the bread and the milk willingly,' said Martin, 'but as for helping me, I doubt if there's anything a little fellow like you can do.'

'There's nothing I *can't* do,' said the elf. 'You're in trouble, aren't you? You're a stonemason, aren't you, and you've work to finish by Hallowe'en that you can't get done in time, eh?'

'I must have been talking to myself,' answered Martin, 'and you must have overheard me.'

'Perhaps I didn't, perhaps I did. Well, luckily for you, I'm a stone worker myself. I can build bridges and make roads. I don't care for church work greatly, for the parsons say hard things about me and my kind, but seeing you're in trouble I'll give you a hand.'

'It's very kind of you,' Martin began, but the elf went on.

'Now if I help you to finish your work by Hallowe'en you must do something for me. Do you hear?'

'And what's that?' said Martin, smiling. He could not help thinking what a strange business it was to be making a bargain with such an odd little creature.

'You must give me your daughter to marry,' said the elf.

'What, my daughter Alison?' asked Martin, hardly believing his ears.

'And why not?' said the elf. 'She's a decent lass, for I've seen her about the countryside. Ah yes, I've seen her when she couldn't see me. She'll do well enough.'

Martin hesitated.

'Well, what do you say?' went on the elf. 'If I help you finish off your work on the new church, will you give me your daughter to marry on Hallowe'en day? Is it a bargain?'

'What if she should refuse?' said Martin. 'She's very particular. She might not fancy being wed to such a little fellow as yourself.'

And then, seeing the elf looking angry, he went on:

'That is, I don't think she's a mind to get married at all just now. What shall I do if she says no?'

'If you make a bargain with me,' answered the elf, 'you must stick to it. There's only one way you can get out of it, though it's scarcely worth the telling.'

'And what's that?'

'If you can guess my name, you can keep your daughter, and you'll never see me alive again.'

Martin said nothing. He got up and went to the larder, bringing out white bread and a bowl of creamy milk.

'Here,' he said, 'have this while I think a bit.'

And as the elf ate the bread and drank the milk, Martin walked up and down the room thinking. How could he make such a bargain? How could he promise his only daughter to such a comical, wizened old fellow? And how would Alison fancy a husband no bigger than her fore-arm? But then, what a help it would be to have the work finished in time! There was barely a week left, and there was no other way of getting it done.

'Perhaps I'm dreaming,' thought Martin. 'Perhaps he can't help me at all. Ah well, why shouldn't I let him have a try? If he *does* manage to do the work for me, there'll be some way out of letting him wed Alison. After all, it shouldn't be such a difficult matter to find out his name. If the worst comes to the worst, I can go and tell the schoolmaster or the priest, and they'll know for sure, with all their deep learning and their books and such stuff. I'll do it.'

So he made the bargain with the elf, and when he had done so he felt a great weight off his mind. The little man's dark eyes twinkled and he smiled a crafty smile as he hopped down off the table.

'Now mind,' he said, 'I'm a man of my word. See that you stick to yours!'

'Never fear, I will,' answered Martin and opened the door quietly.

Before there was time to wish the elf good night, he had scurried out of the door and disappeared in the darkness. For by now the moon had almost set.

Martin laughed to himself at his odd adventure. Then he yawned and went to bed.

Next morning the sun was shining brightly by the time Martin woke up. His daughter was knocking on the door and telling him to hurry and get dressed or he would have cold porridge. So Martin got up, and after breakfast he set off for the church.

What was his surprise to find, neatly piled up waiting for him, ten or a dozen perfectly carved stone blocks! He had certainly not done them himself the day before, and no one else could have carved them except the elf.

'Well I never,' thought Martin. 'So he's going to help me after all. A very clever workman he is too, and no mistake. I couldn't have squared those blocks better myself.'

He took one of the new blocks under one arm and hoisted himself up the scaffolding to the top of the tower. The block exactly fitted the place where it had to go. Leaving it there, Martin went down and mixed some mortar to set the stone hard and keep it in position.

Before long he had cemented all the blocks in place and begun to carve a new one. Then a thought struck him.

'If the little fellow's going to do all the plain stones,' he said to himself, 'why should I trouble myself about them? I'll get on with the figures.'

So he began to shape a piece of stone for the corner of the tower, on which he could carve the second gargoyle. The first had been a fierce dog-like creature with sharp teeth and his tongue hanging out. The next was to be a bird, a long-necked eagle with outspread wings. All the rest of that day Martin worked on the eagle and at sundown he went off home to his cottage.

When he saw his dear daughter Alison making up the fire and beginning to get the supper ready, he suddenly felt sorry for his bargain. What if, after all, the dwarf should really claim her as his bride and carry her off to live in his dark hole under the Ferry

Hill? Perhaps he should tell her all about it, and ask her pardon, and then go off to the hill in search of the elf and tell him the bargain was off. He ought never to have meddled with such matters.

Then he thought to himself: 'But if this is an evil business, why did I catch the little scamp just as I was in need of help? Was he not sent to me in my time of need? What have I to be afraid of? Time to start fretting when Hallowe'en comes.'

He thought no more of the matter and set about cleaning the dust out of his curly hair and getting ready for the good food Alison was preparing.

Next day it was the same. A neat pile of beautifully carved stones was waiting for Martin when he got to the church. Once again he climbed the scaffolding to the top of the high tower and fixed them in place next to the ones he had cemented in the day before. Then he went on with his stone eagle, and so well did he work that by the end of the day he had finished it.

Each day it was the same, and when the master mason came to see how he was doing, he was delighted with Martin's progress.

'Why,' he said, 'now if you'd only work like this all the time, you could be a master mason yourself and have fifty men working for you. And to think you've done all this by yourself! Anyone would think you had evil spirits working for you!'

'Evil spirits don't make good masons,' said Martin, scowling at his master.

'I daresay they don't,' answered the master mason. 'Well, you've three more days, and it looks as if you'll have no trouble to finish the job in time. Good luck to you!'

Next day Martin finished the third gargoyle, and fitted it to the corner where he had left a space for it between the stones shaped by the elf. It was a strange creature, something like a fish, with broad curved fins and wide open mouth.

On the day before Hallowe'en he got to work as usual, and as usual he found the newly squared blocks all ready for him. When he had cemented these in position, he found that only two were still lacking – two blocks and one figure. The work would easily be done in time, that is, if the elf was as good as his word. So he sat down and began to consider what form the fourth gargoyle should take. Perhaps it should be a little demon, he thought. But Sir John might not like that. Perhaps it should be a little dwarf with pointed ears and a crafty smile. But this might offend the elf who had been helping him all this time. So in the end he decided that the last figure should be a dragon. Yes, that was it – a long-necked dragon with a crest over its head, curling teeth, sharp claws, and scales all down its neck. That would remind people of the dragon that Saint George had killed, and nobody could possibly be offended. So without more hesitation, he chose a suitable piece of stone and began chipping away.

He had half-finished the figure when the day began to fade and it was almost time to pack up his tools and set off for home.

All at once there was a little scuffling noise and he turned round to find the elf standing behind him.

'Hello,' exclaimed the mason, 'how you scared me! Where have you been all this time?'

> 'Whence I come and whither I go,
> All may guess but none may know,'

answered the elf.

'Well, you're a neat enough stone-worker,' said Martin, 'if it's you that's been shaping these stone blocks for me.'

'It's me all right,' said the elf. 'Who else, I should like to know? We shall finish the job tomorrow, you and I, and then– then I shall come for my fee. This time tomorrow I'll be with you – an hour before sundown, do you hear?'

'I hear,' said the mason. 'But it's not tomorrow yet. It'll be time enough to claim your fee when the work's done.'

The elf chuckled.

'Well,' he said. 'I just stepped along to remind you of the day. I'll be here tomorrow, never fear. And mind – no tricks.'

Before Martin could answer, the little man had scurried off as fast as he had come, and in two seconds not a sign of him was to be seen.

Martin packed up his tools and made off home with a heavy heart.

That night he hardly slept at all. He tossed and turned on his bed, and his mind was torn with nightmares. He thought he saw a fearsome creature coming for him with the body of a dragon and the face of the little dwarf, and just as it was about to reach him, he woke up, trembling with fright.

At last the morning came. It was Hallowe'en, the day when the work was to be finished, the day when he was to pay the price for all his idleness and folly.

When he got to the church he found the last two blocks of stone waiting for him, just as he knew they would be. He had half-hoped the elf might have forgotten to do his share of the work, so that the bargain would be broken. But there they were, neatly squared and smoothed, as the others had been. Slowly he climbed the scaffolding with one of them under his arm. It seemed to him as heavy as lead. It fitted perfectly, and so did the other. Before the morning was half-through, he had fixed them both in place and begun work on the dragon that was to fill up the last space at the top of the tower.

As Martin cut and scraped, the day wore on. At last, fully half an hour before the time when the elf had promised to come, the figure was finished. There it was, all ready to cement into place. But Martin had not the heart to carry it to the top of the tower. Instead he sat down on a pile of stones and began brooding on what was to come. Should he run away? Should he pretend not to see the elf when he came? Should he strike at him with his hammer or chase him away with stones?

While he was thinking these thoughts, a man came up to him. It was Peter, an old carpenter who had been working with him in the church some time before. He was one of the men who had put in the great beams which supported the roof. Martin did not like him, for he was a hard man to deal with, and at times he was cross-grained and rough in his manner. But just now he seemed in a good humour.

'Why, Martin,' said Peter, 'you've a face as long as a handsaw! Can't you get the work finished in time? I did hear as you was to finish by today or Sir John was going to throw you out.'

'The work's finished,' said Martin, 'or as good as finished.

As for being thrown out of work, I care not whether I am or not.'

'What have you been a-shaping there?' went on Peter. 'Why, I shouldn't wonder if it was your own dragon that's put you out of temper, for it's as life-like and fearsome a dragon as ever I saw! Now that would be a fine thing to scare away evil spirits. I should like to have a figure like that to fix over my door! Then my old woman wouldn't be so mortal scared of demons as she is. But I tell you what, Martin. You've been working too hard. What you need is a night's sport. What do you say to coming out with me next full moon, and scaring up a few of Sir John's birds or a rabbit or two?'

'Perhaps I will and perhaps I won't,' said Martin.

'Only there's one place I won't go,' Peter continued, 'and that's Ferry Hill. I tell you, there's spirits round there. Some folks don't believe in them, but I know better. I'll tell you something I saw last night, though you won't believe me.'

'And what's that?' asked Martin.

'Well, I was a-coming home late, because I'd been over to the

Hall to tighten up a pair of shutters that had shaken loose in the wind. I was coming home late and I passed by the stone quarry on the other side of Ferry Hill. And what should I see – it was getting dark, you understand, and I couldn't make out nothing plain, but –'

'Yes, what did you see?' said Martin impatiently.

'You'll not believe me, but I tell you, dark as it was, I saw a little fellow no longer than my smoothing plane, standing up beside a great block of stone, a-chipping and a-chopping with a little silver chisel and a mallet! Ah, you may laugh, Martin, but I tell you it was one of them dwarfs or spirits or such-like that lives under Ferry Hill. And while he was a-working, he was singing to himself.'

'Did you hear what he sang?' asked Martin.

'I did that,' said Peter. 'He had a little high, quavery voice, and what he sang went something like this. Let me see. "Something or other is my name"; no, that's not it.

> '"Something or other's the name of this same elf.
> Nobody knows it but myself.
> If ever my name on earth is known,
> This same elf shall turn to stone."'

Martin had suddenly become excited.

'What did he say his name was?' he asked eagerly.

'Why, that I can't remember,' said Peter, 'for it meant nothing to me.'

'But you *must* remember!' said Martin. 'Think, think!'

'I can't remember,' repeated the carpenter. 'What's it to you anyhow?'

'Never mind,' said Martin. 'If you can remember what the little fellow's name was, I'll give you anything you want!'

'Well, I *might* call it to mind,' said Peter, 'if I was to think hard enough. But what'll you give me if I think of it, eh? You wouldn't give me that stone dragon you've been a-making now, would you?'

Martin hesitated. If he promised Peter the dragon, how could he make another before the night was out? But what did that matter if only he could find out the elf's name? For he was certain that the little man Peter had seen working in the stone quarry was no other than the very same elf who had been helping him.

'Done!' he cried. 'If you can tell me what the dwarf said, you shall have the gargoyle. There! Now think hard!'

'Give me time,' answered Peter. 'Let me see. "Something's the name of this same elf, Nobody knows it but myself." It's a fine figure of a dragon, that! It'll look terrible fierce over my door, it will. Now, what *did* the little fellow say his name was?'

'Oh, hurry!' said Martin, for the sun was beginning to go down and the shadows were lengthening.

Peter scratched his head and knocked on it with his knuckles. At last he said:

'I've got it – I've got it! "Lob is the name of this same elf." – No, that's not it either. But it was something very like. "Cob" or "Hob", may be. "Nob"! That's it! "Nob is the name of this same elf. Nobody knows it but myself." That's what the little fellow sang. I can hear him now with his chip-chip-chip on the stone and his little high voice –'

He was interrupted by a distant rumble of thunder.

'Hello,' he said, 'storm coming up. I'd best be a-getting home. That was the name all right, so if you're satisfied I'll just take up my fee in this bag and be off with me.'

'Take it, take it!' said Martin, full of joy. He picked up the stone dragon which, though heavy, could easily be carried by a strong man, and gave it to the carpenter.

Peter thanked him, opened his carpenter's bag on the ground and placed the figure safely inside. Then he hoisted it on his shoulder, bade Martin good night and made off.

'Perhaps Sir John will give me two days extra to make another,' said Martin to himself. 'What do I care, so long as I get out of my cursed bargain? And if that fellow Peter has told me wrong, I'll go and fetch the dragon back myself.'

No sooner had he spoken than there was another rumble of thunder, louder than the first, and the sun was darkened by a great cloud. Standing beside Martin was the elf. He hopped on to a block of stone and looked at the mason with his black, glittering eyes.

'Here I am,' he said, 'an hour before sundown, just as I said. Perhaps you thought I wouldn't come?'

Martin said nothing.

'But I've come all right,' the elf went on. 'Have I helped with the work as I said, and is it finished in time?'

'Yes,' said Martin, 'you've helped as you promised, and the work is done.'

'And now for my wages! Are you going to give me my bride, as you agreed, or must I go and take her?'

And the elf chuckled and pointed in the direction of the village.

'No!' shouted Martin. 'I'll not give you my daughter, and you'll not take her! Get you gone where you came from, Master NOB – and never let me see you again! Do you hear – Master NOB?'

At the sound of his name the elf screamed horribly, and leaned out across the stone he was standing on. He waved his fist at Martin, and with an expression of hatred and malice on his little wizened face, he opened his mouth as if to spit poison. As he did so, there was a flash of lightning, a loud peal of thunder, and Martin fell senseless to the ground.

Then the thunder-storm passed, and Martin came to himself, his face and hands splashed with rain. There in front of him, as if carved in stone, was the figure of the elf just as Martin had last seen him, his mouth open and his face twisted with rage. Then he thought of the words of the elf's song:

> 'If ever my name on earth is known,
> This same elf shall turn to stone.'

In what was left of the daylight, Martin saw that the elf, turned to stone, was now part of the block on which he had been standing. It was the very same size as that on which he had carved the dragon. Now he had another gargoyle instead – a very different one! Instead of the scaly dragon with a crest and sharp claws, there was the figure of a little, evil-faced dwarf with pointed cap and open mouth.

'That'll scare away the evil spirits,' said Martin to himself as he carried the figure to the top of the tower. It fitted exactly. Quickly he cemented the gargoyle in its place, put a sack over it so that the mortar would not spoil with the rain, and went off home in the gathering darkness.

That is the story which is told of the fourth gargoyle on the tower of Elphinstone Church. And when Sir John Tilbury, the old, rich merchant, saw Martin's handiwork, he was especially struck by the figure of the elf.

'Why,' said he, 'the village shall be named after that same carving, for I never saw so good a one before. It shall be called "Elf-in-Stone", for that's what all travellers to this place will see when they raise their heads to the tower – an Elf in stone.'

In this way Martin the mason kept both his daughter and his job, and the village where he lived got a new church and a new name.

Simple Jack

Jack lived with his mother in a cottage beside a common. He was the laziest boy in the world. His mother earned a living for them both by spinning, and when she wasn't spinning she was washing or mending, and when she wasn't washing or mending she was getting a meal ready. But all Jack would do was to sit under the apple tree in summer sucking grasses, and in the chimney corner in winter keeping his toes warm.

At last his mother could put up with it no longer.

'Out you go,' said she one fine Monday morning. 'Out you go, and earn yourself a living or you shan't stay here any more. You're old enough to get work for yourself now, so don't come back till you've made some money to help pay for the food you eat!'

Slowly Jack got up from his seat by the fire and went out. He hired himself to a farmer, and by the end of the day he had earned sixpence. Holding it in his hand, he started for home; but, crossing over a brook, he slipped on a wet stone and dropped the sixpence. It was nowhere to be found. There was nothing for it but to go home and tell his mother what had happened.

'Why, you stupid boy!' said his mother. 'I could have done with sixpence, but now you've lost it. You should have put it in your pocket. Then you'd have kept it safe and sound. See you if you can do better tomorrow.'

Well, on Tuesday morning Jack went off once more, though he would rather have sat by the fire all day. This time he hired himself to a dairyman, and at the end of the day he was given a pail of milk for wages. So remembering what his mother had said, he emptied the pail into the pocket of his coat and began to jog along home. Of course the milk was all wasted, and his clothes were soaked into the bargain.

'Why, you silly, good-for-nothing scamp!' cried his mother, when he told her what had happened. 'We could have done with some nice new milk for supper, but now there's none – thanks to your foolishness. You should have carried the pail on your head, then you would have brought it home safe and sound.'

On Wednesday morning Jack went off again to work for the farmer, and for his day's work the farmer gave him a fine pat of butter.

'Now, what did she tell me to do with it?' thought Jack. Then he remembered. He clapped the butter on top of his head and started for home. But it was a warm evening, and soon the butter got stuck in his hair and ran down behind his ears, and some of it fell to the ground, and all of it was spoilt.

Jack's mother was angrier than ever.

'It's too bad!' she said. 'I could have done with some good

dairy butter if you hadn't gone and spoilt it all. What a donkey you are! Whatever did you put it on your head for? You should have carried it in your hand.'

Well, on Thursday morning Jack set off once more, trudging away across the common to see a baker in the village; and all day he worked for the baker, and the baker gave him nothing but a black cat for his day's work. He had too many cats in the bakery and was glad to get rid of one.

When he got home, he had nothing at all to show for his day's work except a pair of hands covered all over with bites and scratches.

'What did you get today?' asked Jack's mother.

'Why, the baker gave me a black cat, mother,' said Jack, 'and I carried her in my hands like you told me yesterday, and she scratched me till I had to let her go.'

'Deary me, deary me!' said his mother. 'Aren't you the stupidest ninny ever born? You shouldn't have tried to carry a cat home in your hands. You should have tied a string round her neck and pulled her along after you. It's very vexing,' she went on. 'We could have done with a good cat to keep the mice from the larder!'

On Friday morning Jack went off to the butcher's shop and hired himself to the butcher for the day. Now the butcher was a kind man and knew that Jack's mother was poor, so at the end of the day he gave Jack a leg of good lean mutton. Jack thanked the butcher and left the shop. He thought very carefully about what his mother had told him the day before, and this time he was determined to make no mistake. So he took a piece of string from his pocket and pulled the meat along behind him in the road.

When she saw the meat, all dirty and spoilt, Jack's mother was more annoyed than ever.

'Oh, you dunderhead!' she cried. 'When *will* you learn sense? We could have done with a fine lean leg of mutton for dinner tomorrow and you've as good as thrown it away! Fancy bringing it home like that!'

'But what *should* I have done, mother?' Jack asked.

'If you'd had two penn'orth of common sense, you'd have lifted it on your shoulder and carried it home like that. Be off to bed with you, for there's not a bite of supper in the house. The way you're going on, we shall both starve, and that's the truth!'

Well, next morning was Saturday, and once more Jack set out to see what he could earn. He hired himself to a cowman that he knew, and at the end of the day the cowman gave him a donkey. So remembering once more what his mother had told him, Jack hoisted the donkey on to his shoulders, and staggered off home. The animal gave poor Jack a great deal of trouble, for it did not like being carried upside down on his shoulders. However, Jack was determined to get home safely *this* time, and not lose his day's wages. So he grasped the donkey's legs with all his strength and took no notice of its braying and kicking.

Now it so happened that in a great house beside the high road lived a rich man, and he had one beautiful daughter who was both deaf and dumb. She had never heard or spoken a word in all her life. But the doctor had told her father that, if the girl could be made to laugh, she might be cured. And the rich man had spent years and years trying to make his beautiful daughter laugh, but the harder he tried the sadder she looked, till everyone gave up hope of ever having her cured.

As Jack was passing the house with the donkey upside down on his back, it happened that the girl was looking out of an upstairs window. Never had she seen such a thing in all her life! There must surely be nothing funnier in the world than to see a great country lad staggering along the road with a donkey kicking and braying upside down on his back: at first the girl could not believe her eyes, and then she began to smile, and then her smile grew broader and broader until she laughed out loud; she laughed so loud and long that the tears came to her eyes, and scarcely knowing what she was doing, she called out to everyone in the house:

'Oh, c-come and look! J-just come and look! Did you ever see such a thing? It's the funniest thing you ever saw!'

Well, the girl's father and all their friends were delighted that at last the girl had spoken, and they were so pleased that they ran

out into the road and called Jack inside. So in he went, donkey and all, and the girl was so pleased with him that she wouldn't let him go.

Nothing would please the rich man's daughter but that she should marry Jack and have him to live with for always. And very happy they were in a great house which the rich man bought for them. They kept the donkey in a field at the back of the house, and Jack's mother came to live with them for the rest of her life. Jack became a fine gentleman and had servants to wait on him and see that he never did any more work from that time on.

Rapunzel

There was once a poor couple who lived in a cottage at the edge of a wood. At the back of the cottage was a little window which looked out over a high stone wall. Beyond the wall was a most beautiful garden, where grew all manner of flowers and herbs. In the trees the birds sang sweetly all day long, and in the middle of a green lawn a sparkling fountain played. The couple had never seen a garden like this. But they had not been inside it, for it belonged to a cruel witch named Gothel.

Now in that garden there grew a herb called rampion, which is used for making salads. In that country it was known as *rapunzel*.

'Ah, husband,' sighed the poor woman one day as she looked out of the window, 'I don't feel well, but I believe I would get better if only I had some of that rampion to eat.'

The poor man was distressed to see his wife ill, and he determined to get her some of the herb, cost what it might. So that evening, when the witch was not to be seen in her garden, he climbed over the wall and seized a handful of the rampion. Then he scrambled back and gave it to his wife. When she had eaten it, she felt better.

But next day it was just the same.

'Oh, I shall die,' said she, 'if I can't have more of that herb.'

And indeed she looked so pale and ill that her husband went once more into the garden and took a bunch of the rampion. He was just going to climb back over the wall when the witch came and saw him.

'Aha!' she cried. 'What are you doing in my garden?

Why do you come here in the dark and steal my magic herbs?'

'Oh, madam,' said the poor man, 'my wife is very ill. She says that, if she can't get this herb to make into a salad, she will die. Please, I beg you, let me keep it.'

At this the witch seemed to take pity on the man.

'Very well,' she said, 'you may keep it. You have no children yet, but soon your wife is to have a daughter. In payment for the rampion, you must allow me to have the child when it is born!'

What could the poor man do but agree? For he thought that otherwise his wife would die, and he would have no one left in the world.

So every evening he went into the witch's garden for a bunch of the herb his wife so much desired. She seemed to get better every day, and at last her little girl was born.

Almost immediately the cruel witch appeared at her bedside and demanded the baby. So the poor couple were obliged to give up their only child. Gothel laughed with glee and took the baby away, to bring up as her own. She named her Rapunzel after the herb as it was called in those parts. Every day the child grew stronger, until she could be seen playing in the witch's beautiful garden. Sometimes her parents caught a glimpse of her running amid the flowerbeds, chasing a butterfly or calling to the birds, while her golden hair waved behind her in the breeze. And it seemed to the poor couple that their daughter was more beautiful than any of the flowers in the garden.

But when Rapunzel was twelve years old, the cruel witch took her away from the garden and shut her in a tall, dark tower in the middle of a forest. Now this tower was built of stone and had no door and no stairs, but only a window at the top. Hour after hour Rapunzel would sit at the window looking out on the forest or singing to herself. And when the witch wanted to get to her, she would call 'Rapunzel, Rapunzel, let down your long hair.' The girl's hair was so long and fine, like spun gold, that it came nearly to the ground, and was as strong as a cord. She would twist it round one of the bars of the window, and the witch would climb up it like a ladder. Then, when she had finished with Rapunzel and given her her food, she would climb down again by the strands of gold hair, which Rapunzel would then draw up again into her room at the top of the tower. It was a lonely life, but the girl sang to keep herself happy.

So the years passed. Rapunzel grew into a fair and graceful maiden, and the witch hated her beauty and vowed she would keep her in the high tower for ever.

One day, some years later, it happened that the King's son, who had strayed from his companions while hunting, passed by the stone tower when Rapunzel was singing to herself in her lonely room. He stopped and listened, for never had he heard so beautiful a voice. This is what the voice was singing:

'Bird of the air, bird in the tree,
Sing your happiest song to me.
Bird in the tree, bird of the air,
Sing me a song of love or care.
Sing your best,
And I will give you a golden hair,
To line your nest.'

The young Prince longed to know who it was who sang with such a clear, lovely voice, and he rode up to the tower, but nowhere could he find a door; and even if he had found a door, he could not have climbed up the tower, for there were no stairs. So cunningly had the cruel witch Gothel imprisoned the girl. The Prince could do nothing but turn his horse's head and ride home.

Next day he came again, so enchanted was he by the sound of Rapunzel's voice, and every day he came, but never could he find a way into the tall tower.

Then one day he was just approaching it when he saw the witch a little way ahead of him. He hid behind a tree to see what she did.

'Rapunzel, Rapunzel,' called the witch, 'let down your long hair!'

Then the Prince was astonished to see a long rope of spun gold being twisted round one of the bars of the window and let down to the ground. Next, he saw Gothel grasp it with her two bony hands and climb nimbly to the window and squeeze through.

'Aha!' thought he. 'That is how to get into the tower where the lady sings!'

So he rode home, and next day he came again towards evening, when he thought the witch would be out of sight. He stood below the window and called softly, 'Rapunzel, Rapunzel, let down your long hair.'

He waited a moment, then the same thing happened as he had seen the day before. The long coil of gold hair fell almost to his feet; so, looking round to see that the witch was nowhere near, he climbed swiftly to the top of the tower and got in through the window.

At first Rapunzel was frightened to see the strange young man instead of the old witch. But he spoke to her in friendly tones, and she thought he was kinder and gentler than Gothel.

'Don't be afraid, sweet maiden,' said the King's son. 'I do not come to harm you. For many days I have listened to the sound of your voice as you sing at the window, and at last I have come to see you.'

So he sat down, and they talked, and the Prince told Rapunzel of the world outside the tower, and of the great country over which his father the King ruled.

He came to see her every evening, until one day he said to her:

'Rapunzel, I am a Prince, and I wish no one but yourself to be my Princess. Will you marry me?'

Rapunzel, who loved him dearly, answered 'Yes,' and put her hand in his. Then he told her that as soon as he could get her out of the stone tower, he would make her his wife.

'Every day when you come to see me,' said Rapunzel, 'bring me a skein of silk. Then I shall weave a ladder, and with this I shall escape out of the window and get safely to the ground.'

The Prince did as she said. Every evening, when the witch was nowhere to be seen, he came to the tower and climbed up to Rapunzel and gave her a skein of silk, so that before long she had almost woven the ladder for her escape.

The witch Gothel knew nothing of this until one unlucky day Rapunzel said to her:

'Tell me, Gothel, how is it that when you climb up my hair, you are so much heavier than the young Prince who visits me? Why, he seems to fly up in no time.'

Now this was a foolish thing to say, but Rapunzel did not know how angry the witch would be.

'Oh, you wicked girl!' screamed Gothel. 'So you have visitors, have you? It was not for that that I shut you in this tower. Well, I shall put an end to your tricks, you deceitful child!'

So she took out her sharp scissors and snip-snap! in a moment she had cut off all Rapunzel's beautiful hair. Next, she spirited her from the tower and led her away to a wild and dreary wilderness where there was nothing but dead trees and scrub growing amidst the dry stones. She left Rapunzel there to wander about looking for roots and berries to keep herself from starving.

Then Gothel returned to the tower and fixed Rapunzel's long coil of hair to the bar of the window, and waited. When the Prince came and called 'Rapunzel, Rapunzel, let down your long hair,' she threw down the golden coil at his feet. Lightly he climbed to the window, expecting to see the sweet face of his love, Rapunzel. Instead, he saw the cruel mocking eyes of the witch Gothel.

'So you are the Prince who comes sneaking through the forest to see the little bird in the stone cage!' cried the witch in triumph. 'Well, the bird has flown, my beauty, and you will never see her again! Instead, the old cat will scratch out your eyes, you meddling thief!'

'Never!' cried the Prince in anger and despair.

So saying, he leapt from the window and fell upon the ground. But he was not killed, only bruised and shaken, for he had fallen into some thorn bushes. Alas! the thorns stuck in his eyes and, blinded, he wandered away, almost mad with grief and pain.

For days he stumbled through the woods, calling upon his lost Rapunzel, blundering here, there and everywhere in his blindness; but no one heard him, and he believed he must soon die from hunger and weariness.

Rapunzel, meanwhile, struggled on through the stony desert that Gothel had banished her to. She seemed to go round and round in circles, for there was no way out. There was scarcely anything to eat or drink, and no birds sang to cheer her. She almost ceased to think of her Prince, whom she would never see again. Her hair, which the cruel Gothel had snipped off, began to grow again, but her clothes were ragged, and her body thin and starved, so that anyone who had seen her before would no longer recognize her. One day, when the sun shone, she tried to cheer herself by singing in a voice now small and shaking, and yet with something of its old sweetness:

'Bird of the air, bird in the tree,
Sing your happiest song to me.
Bird in the tree, bird of the air,
Sing me a song of love or care.'

The wind carried the notes of her song across the wilderness to the ears of the Prince, who, almost dead from weakness and despair, had at last reached the place where Rapunzel wandered.

'What is that sound?' he cried feebly. 'Surely that is her voice – or do I imagine it?'

Blindly he stumbled towards the place where the sound seemed to be, calling out, as best he could, 'Rapunzel, Rapunzel, where are you?'

Then she saw him. She ran towards him, crying 'My Prince, is it you? Have you found me at last?'

Then she saw that he was blind. She ran to him and put her arms about him; and the Prince, so overcome with joy and faint from thirst and hunger, dropped at her feet. The girl wept to see him in such a sorry state; and as she looked down at his tired, thin face, the tears fell from her eyes on to his. Rapunzel's tears entered his eyes, and he received his sight back again. He looked up at her face and saw her almost as clearly as he had seen her when first he climbed up her golden hair to the window in the high tower.

Somehow they found their way out of the dreary wilderness, and the first thing they did was to go to the King's palace; and the King knew all about Rapunzel's mother and father, and how they had had to give up their only child to the cruel witch. So the poor man and his wife were sent for, and there was great rejoicing. Afterwards, the Prince and Rapunzel were married, and a great and solemn feast was held.

As for Gothel, they shut her up in her own high tower and kept her there. But the tower was struck by lightning in a great storm and crashed to the ground. And the witch vanished, to be seen no more. Some say she was destroyed by lightning; others, that she had flown away on a black cloud. So her garden was deserted, and after a time it was given to the poor man and woman, Rapunzel's parents, who walked in it whenever they wished, without fear or hindrance.

The Secret Shoemakers

'Well, my dear,' said old Gregory the shoemaker to his wife Joan, 'that's the end of the leather. I've cut out my last pair of shoes, and I'll sew them in the morning. Now I'll go to bed, for I'm tired.'

'What shall we do then?' asked Joan anxiously. 'Have you nothing to buy more leather with?'

'You know we've no money for leather.'

'Can't you borrow some leather from a brother shoemaker?'

'I've borrowed all I can. Times are bad. Leather's too dear. It's all being bought to make saddles and bridles for horses to take men to the war. I'm not a saddler. I'm too old to learn a new trade. I daresay we'll get along by a bit of mending and cobbling. It's no good worrying. I'm off to bed.'

But Gregory and Joan were both worried. They had little enough to live on, nothing for new clothes, and soon the winter would be upon them and they would have to buy wood for the stove. Gregory was a fine cobbler, one of the best, but he had lost trade through a long illness. People had gone elsewhere for new shoes. Still, the old shoemaker was not one to complain about what couldn't be helped. He laid out the leather pieces on his bench in the workshop, ready to be stitched in the morning, and soon he was fast asleep in the little attic bedroom.

Next morning Gregory was amazed to find on his work bench, not a pile of leather pieces but a pair of shoes, quite finished and perfectly stitched together with neat, regular stitches.

He called his wife, and together they looked at the shoes in astonishment.

'We've got secret helpers,' said the shoemaker. 'There's no doubt of it. I couldn't do work like that in a whole week, let alone one night.'

As soon as the shop was open, customers began to come in for shoes they had left to be mended. Then towards midday a fine lady came in with her maid. She needed a pair of shoes. She could not wait to have them made to measure, as she was going on a journey that very day. Great was her delight when she found that the new shoes fitted perfectly. She was so pleased with the fine workmanship that she gave Gregory over and above what he asked for them. She had been an old customer before his illness and she knew that times were bad.

With the money she paid, Gregory hurried off to the dealer and bought enough leather for two new pairs of shoes. He gave Joan the money that was left over to buy food.

That evening he cut out two more pairs of shoes and put the pieces on the bench before going to bed. He was quite ready to begin stitching them in the morning, for he hardly dared to hope that his secret helpers would come a second night.

But sure enough, as soon as the shoemaker came downstairs in the morning, he found two pairs of finished shoes on his bench, as finely and perfectly stitched as the first pair. He was not long in finding customers for these new pairs, and with the money he got for them he was able to buy leather for four fresh pairs. With his usual skill he cut them out and left the pieces on his bench to be stitched together next day. But once more Gregory and Joan were overjoyed to find the finished shoes placed neatly on the bench next morning.

So it went on. Each night the shoemaker left a number of pairs of shoes ready to be stitched together by his secret friends, and every morning he found them finished and ready to be sold. Gregory and his wife began to be prosperous and to live comfortably as they had done in the old days. Joan had a new winter dress, and there was plenty of good dry wood to keep them warm. At last Joan said to her husband, 'Gregory, I have a mind to see who it is that helps us in the night.'

'Better leave well alone,' said her husband, though, truth to tell, he too had been wondering.

'Perhaps there is something we could do to repay them,' answered his wife. 'They may be in need of something.'

'My dear, you are right. Tonight let us leave a candle alight in the workshop and hide behind those old clothes that hang against the wall. Then we shall get to the bottom of this mystery.'

And so they did. Gregory and Joan sat on a bench against the wall, peeping out between the folds of the clothes that hid them from sight. For a long time nothing happened. At last they heard the chimes of midnight sound sleepily through the cold night air. A moment later, as if from nowhere, and with scarcely a rustle, appeared two little men. Without a word to each other they hopped on to the shoemaker's bench, sat down cross-legged, took up the leather pieces, needle and thread, and began stitching away. Never had Gregory seen such nimble fingers. The needles flashed like sparks in the candlelight, and the thread flew in and out, in and out, as if by magic.

Indeed, the little men must certainly have had magical power, for no human being could work so fast and so finely.

The shoemaker and his wife scarcely breathed, for they did not wish to scare the little men. But they noticed that these two secret shoemakers were dressed only in the thinnest of rags, torn and patched, and that their thin bodies showed through the holes and tatters in a manner piteous to see. Now and again they shivered, but not for a moment did they stop working until all the shoes were finished and ready. Then they tidied up the needles and thread, placed the shoes neatly in pairs along the bench, and vanished as silently as they had come. When Gregory and Joan came out of hiding, their secret helpers were nowhere to be seen.

'Those poor little elves,' said Joan. 'Did you see how miserably they were clothed?'

'Did you see how cold they were this frosty night?' said

Gregory, who was a little cold himself, inspite of his warm clothes.

'I tell you what, husband,' said Joan. 'Instead of giving them work tonight, let us make them some clothes. We have plenty of shoes in stock, thanks to them.'

'Yes, indeed,' agreed Gregory. 'We scarcely need their help any more. My work is so highly prized that I have all the trade I want and more. Besides, I am strong and well and can easily look after our needs without help. This big stock of leather will last us through the winter, and perhaps we could even afford to take a little holiday.'

So it was agreed. Joan spent all day making two little shirts of warm flannel, two pairs of trousers, two pairs of woollen stockings and two little caps to protect the elves' heads. Gregory made two neat pairs of shoes out of soft red leather. At night they left some supper for the elves and a bit of fire in the grate. Then they went to bed, for they were very tired after their day's work. They had had little sleep the night before.

When morning came, Gregory and Joan went downstairs to see what had become of their presents. The fire was out, the food was eaten, and there was no sign of the little clothes they had made the day before.

The shoemaker and his wife never saw their secret helpers

again, and the little men did not come, for there was no need of them. What had happened in the night was this.

As soon as the elves arrived in the workshop, promptly at midnight, they had skipped on to the bench to begin work. But they were surprised and delighted to find the two suits of clothes and the two pairs of shoes laid out for them. Immediately they danced with joy, threw their old rags into the fire and put on the new clothes. Then they sat down to supper on the hearth and finished every scrap the good shoemaker's wife had left them.

'Now,' cried one elf to the other, 'we have fine suits of warm clothes. We can live like gentlemen at last, and need do no more shoemaking.'

So away they skipped, vanishing as they had come, and not a sign did they leave except two empty bowls, each with a spoon in it.

Little Monday

There was once a baker, who lived with his wife and their two children in a house on the edge of a town. He baked all the bread for the people in that part of the town, and twice a week he made cakes. His wife cooked and sewed and washed for her family, and on market-days she went into town to buy everything that was needed for the household.

They had two children and no more. Tom was about eleven years old and his sister was eight. Although she was only eight, Frances was fond of sewing and had already become quite clever. She would mend for her mother or make simple things such as dusters. Best of all she liked to make clothes for her dolls out of pieces of bright curtain material which her mother did not want. Tom helped his father in the bakery, which was warm and dark and smelt of bread; or else he did odd jobs in the garden or about the house, and in the evenings he would sit at a corner of the big table in the living-room and do his lessons.

Tom and Frances did not play much with other children – not because they did not like them, but because there were not many children of their age in that part of the town. Besides, they were very fond of each other and would play happily together for hours. Tom would mend his sister's dolls if their arms and legs came loose, as they sometimes did; and Frances would help Tom with his toy soldiers and his trains. In the fine weather they would go off together to the fields outside the town.

As for the baker, he was a very busy man who did not say much and was nearly always covered with flour and smelt of warm, crisp, new bread. When his work was done, he would come in and sit in a high, hard chair and put on his steel spectacles and read the newspaper or the Bible or some other book.

It was rather a serious family, you might say, but all four of them were happy. None of them seemed to want the bright lights of the town in the evening, or smart clothes, or money to jingle in their pockets. They were not rich, but they did not spend very much, and the baker saved a good deal of what he earned.

The house was small but comfortable, and the baker's wife kept it clean and tidy. Sometimes, but not very often, they had friends in to tea on Sunday; and sometimes the baker's wife would have a chat with her neighbour over the garden wall. Occasionally the baker would go to the public house along the road for a drink and a smoke and to talk about the weather or the state of the country with his fellow-tradesmen.

One very wet evening in the late autumn the baker's family were all sitting round the fire in the living-room. The tea things had been cleared away and washed up, and the table had been pulled near the fire. It was cold as well as wet. The big oil-lamp stood in the middle of the table, casting its glow on Tom's school books and on his mother's pile of mending. Frances was making a nightdress for one of her dolls out of a piece of an old sheet. The baker was sitting in his high-backed chair reading the newspaper.

'A terrible evening,' the baker's wife said for the third or fourth time. 'I don't remember such an evening for goodness knows how long.'

Nobody said anything. Indeed it was difficult to talk because of the noise of the rain on the roof and the gusty wind howling in the chimney and rattling the window-frames.

A few minutes later the baker took his pipe from his mouth and said:

'Do you think you could fasten that window a little tighter, Tom, my boy? There's a draught a-blowing down my neck.'

Tom did as he was told. Again the wind howled, and now the window did not rattle so much. But there was soon a rattling at the door instead.

'Dear me, dear me,' said the baker. 'It's a terrible bad wind. I don't remember such a wind for goodness knows how long. I shall have to go and shut down my bakehouse oven or 'twill be out before morning.'

He knocked his pipe out on the hearth, put down his newspaper and got up. There was another gust of wind and even more rain on the roof. Then the door rattled again. Everyone sat up and listened, for a voice was distinctly heard saying:

'Let me in! Oh, please let me in!'

The baker went to the door and opened it.

On the doorstep was a very small girl with only a thin dress to cover her, a pair of ragged black stockings and worn-out shoes, and no hat or coat. The rain was pouring from her clothes and from her tangled black hair, which hung in streaks down her pale, wet face. She was shivering with cold and every inch of her thin body seemed to be rattling with fear and streaming with water.

'Come in, child,' said the baker. 'Come in and let's get the door a-closed before we be all blown away.'

He pulled the little girl across the threshold, where she stood dripping on the doormat while they all looked at her.

'Come away and get beside the fire,' said the baker's wife. She put down her mending and led the child to the fire. Puddles began to form on the hearth-rug.

'Best get her dry,' said the baker, 'then we can give her something to eat; then maybe she won't catch her death of cold.'

The baker's wife took her into the kitchen, dried her and gave her some warm clothes of Frances' instead of her own sopping rags. These were put straight into the sink to be washed. Then the little girl was given a seat at the table nearest the fire, and the baker brought her a piece of meat pie and some bread and butter and a mug of hot milk with sugar in it. The little girl ate hungrily and all the time she said nothing.

'Now then,' said the baker, when she had finished her meal, 'let's have a little talk. For I suppose you *can* talk, my dear?'

'Oh yes,' said the little girl brightly. 'I can talk plenty when I want to.'

Then she added 'But I don't want to sometimes.'

And she laughed in a queer sort of way without smiling.

She was a funny-looking urchin, the baker's wife was thinking. How very plain she was with her little close-set eyes and dark straight hair and wide mouth showing most of her teeth.

'Well, perhaps you'll tell us what your name is?' went on the baker.

'Monday,' said the little girl.

'I know 'tis Monday,' said the baker. 'I know 'tis Monday, 'cos 'twas Sunday yesterday, but I asked you your name.'

Again the little girl laughed without smiling.

'That *is* my name,' she said. 'I'm called Monday because it was on a Monday I was born. My mother told me.'

'What a funny name,' said Frances. Then she thought this might sound rude, so she said: 'I mean, what a *queer* name. I've never heard it before. How old are you?'

'Nine or ten,' said Monday. 'Ten or nine – I can't remember which.'

She did not look nine or ten, because she was so very small – smaller than Frances, in fact. But she might have been just nine, thought the baker's wife.

'Where's your mother now, little Monday?' said the baker. 'You must tell us where she lives, for we'll have to be taking you back there when this rain stops.'

'I haven't a mother,' said the little girl. 'No, nor a father; and I don't live *any*where. You'll just have to keep me, I'm afraid.'

This surprised everyone. They all stopped for a minute and thought.

'If you haven't got a mother,' said Tom, 'how could she tell you when you were born? You said you knew you were born on a Monday because your mother said so.'

'That's right,' said the baker's wife, proud of her son's cleverness.

'Oh, that was a long time ago,' said Monday. 'I haven't got a mother *now*. That's what I meant.'

It seemed there was nothing to be done that night except to

keep little Monday and put her to bed. Then in the morning the baker could go to the police and find out what was to be done with her. So she was put to bed with Frances, who was very interested in her new companion but was not quite sure whether she liked her.

In the morning the baker remembered that owing to the arrival of little Monday he had forgotten to attend to the oven the night before. In the strong wind it had burnt out. Instead of going to the town to see the police, he had to light the stove again, and this made him late with his baking. His wife had to dry and clean the mats on which Monday had stood when she was dripping with rain the night before. Tom said at breakfast:

'She's a funny little thing, isn't she? Don't know that we want her living here.'

But Frances was not quite so sure.

'Perhaps she'll play with me when I get in from school before you.'

Then Monday came in for her breakfast, and they stopped talking.

Before tea-time, the baker had been into town and his wife had had several talks with the neighbours. But nobody had the least idea whom little Monday belonged to or where she came from. Monday herself did not seem to know either. She had been living, she said, with some other people in a house a long way away, and last night they had said very unkind things to her about the trouble she was causing them, so she had slipped out when they were not looking and walked into town through the rain.

'Perhaps these other people will put up a notice saying you are lost,' said the baker's wife, 'or perhaps they'll come looking for you themselves.'

'I don't think so,' said Monday. 'They didn't like me much.'

So it was decided that Monday should stay with the baker's family for the time being, as long as she promised not to make too much trouble and to help all she could.

After tea she agreed to help dry up the tea things. Except for breaking a cup and saucer, she did this very well and quite willingly. Then she offered to help Frances make her doll's nightdress.

'Can you sew?' asked Frances.

'Oh yes,' said Monday, 'give it to me. I'll show you.'

She took the sewing and sat by the fire and got on with it while Frances undressed her dolls for bed. But when Monday finished sewing, it was found that she had stitched up the ends of the sleeves so that the dolls could not get their arms through. The nightdress looked so funny that everyone laughed. The baker's wife had to unpick the stitches and finish the work herself. Monday laughed too in that queer way of hers, and Frances, though she had laughed, was not at all sure that she was pleased.

Next day the baker's wife went to see Frances' teacher, and it was agreed that Monday should go to school. But Monday refused to go. Nothing would make her. The baker's wife took her along to the school, and no sooner had she returned home than little Monday followed her into the house.

'That's a silly place,' said Monday. 'I couldn't possibly stay there.'

Try as she would, the baker's wife could not make Monday stay at school, so in the end she allowed her to spend her time at home, running round and doing odd jobs, playing in the garden and chasing stray cats. She went into the bakehouse with the baker, but she burnt her fingers and got in the way, and in the end he had to forbid her to go there again.

One evening Tom left his lesson books open on the table with a bottle of ink and a pen beside them. Frances was helping her mother in the kitchen and the baker was in the bakehouse mixing the cakes for the following day. When Tom came back, he found that Monday had been helping him with his lessons and had accidentally spilt ink all over his clean page. He was very angry, very angry indeed.

'What did you go and do that for?' he said. 'Now I shall have to tear out the page and start all over again.'

'I was only trying to help. Don't be cross with me, Tom, *please*,' she begged.

All the same Tom was angry.

'You needn't do it again now,' said Monday. 'It's Saturday tomorrow, so you can play. Come on, let's get the trains out. We can have a wonderful game while Francie's in the kitchen.'

So they got the trains out, and Monday had all sorts of ideas for new and interesting games with them. Soon Frances came in from the kitchen.

'Oh, you might have waited for me,' she said. 'You know I love playing with the trains.'

'Well, you can play now,' said Tom. 'Come on, let's put the rails together and get out the goods vans.'

But now Monday no longer wanted to play; she sat in a corner and made nasty remarks.

When the baker came in from his work, she went up to him and said:

'You'll be terribly cross with me, I'm afraid.'

'Oh dear,' said the baker, 'and why should I be cross with you, eh?'

He sat down by the fireplace. Monday did not answer his question but got up on his knee and said:

'I'm sorry you're going to be cross with me because then you won't want to sing to us.'

'Oh, I'm a-going to sing to you, am I?' asked the baker. 'What makes you think I can sing, eh?'

'Oh, but you can,' said Monday. 'I've heard you singing to yourself in the bakehouse when you thought nobody was listening.'

'And what were you a-doing in the bakehouse?' asked the baker. 'I thought I told you you weren't to go there any more.'

'I didn't think you meant it,' said Monday, grinning and showing all her teeth. 'Besides, how could I sweep up the floor if I didn't go in?'

'So it's you who's been a-sweeping up my floor,' said the baker. 'Well, may I ask you, did you see my pipe by any chance, for I think it fell out of my pocket when I was a-stooping down by the oven.'

'Yes,' said Monday, 'I did see your pipe, and I swept it up and threw it into the fire. I tried to get it out but I was too late, and I saw it burning there along with the other rubbish.'

'Well, you're the stupidest, wastefullest little urchin I've ever seen,' said the baker, getting angry. 'What did you want to come a-interfering in my bakehouse at all for, after I'd told ye not to, I should like to know?'

'I'm terribly sorry,' said Monday, the tears beginning to show in her little black eyes. 'I'm terribly sorry, truly I am. Anyway,' she went on, as the baker's wife came in from the kitchen, 'you shouldn't smoke that nasty dirty pipe. Mother says so; I've heard her say so lots of times.'

'Did you say that?' said the baker angrily, turning to his wife.

'Maybe I did, maybe I didn't,' said the baker's wife. 'What's it to do with *her* whether I said it or not?'

By this time Frances and Tom were quarrelling about what to play, because Frances wanted to play with the trains, while Tom was tired of them.

'No,' said Tom. 'I'm going to put them away, and then I'm going to read.'

'I'll help you, Tom,' said Monday.

'No,' said Frances, 'I'll help. Let me, Tom, please.'

'I helped get them out,' said Monday.

'I want to help put them away,' said Frances.

'You shan't,' said Monday, 'I want to.'

Then Frances began to cry.

'There you are,' said the baker's wife, now thoroughly annoyed with her husband and her children. 'Now look what you've done. You've made Francie cry. Never mind what the horrid little girl says, my duck. You shall help Tom put the trains away, so you shall.'

Monday was by now sitting in the middle of the floor trying to fit an engine and a railway-signal into a cardboard box. She began to laugh.

'As for you,' went on the baker's wife, turning to Monday, 'you're a troublemaker, that's what you are – nothing but a nasty, low-down, mean, sneaking, impudent little trouble-maker!'

Monday laughed still louder. How she was enjoying herself!

'I love trouble,' said little Monday between her laughs. 'Oh, I love it, I love it, I *love* it!'

'Be quiet, you nasty little too-clever-by-half –'

'I do so love trouble! Don't you, Tom? I can't help it, I'm made that way.'

So Monday went on laughing, and the baker's wife scolded, Frances cried, the baker tried to find himself another pipe, and Tom went on putting the trains away; and this wasn't easy because little Monday was rolling about in the middle of the room and getting in the way.

Presently the noise died down and everyone felt rather un-happy. Monday got up from the floor and went across to the baker and put her elbows on his knees and looked up at him with her ugly little face.

'Now what about that song?' she asked. 'You were going to sing to us. Oh, please sing to us.'

'Oh yes, Dad, *do*!' said Frances, wiping away her tears.

The baker didn't want to sing to them, but it seemed the best thing to do. So he sat Frances on one knee and Monday on the other and put his arms round their middles.

'I don't know any smart songs,' he said. 'I can't remember the words; but scraps as I know I'll sing to you gladly, if it'll keep you quiet and stop you for ever fuming and mischief-making.'

And in a rather rusty voice the baker began to sing.

'Now comes the spring with flowers so bright,
    The birds have long been woken.
The Christmas tree has withered away,
    And Christmas toys are broken.
      Fala, fala!
Now is this not the silliest song,
    That ever was sung or spoken?'

The baker stopped for a moment to think.

'What a silly song!' said Monday.

'Never mind,' said Tom, who had now packed up his trains and drawn near to listen. 'Go on, Dad.'

The baker cleared his throat and went on.

'I gave to my true love a cup,
  'Twas but a foolish token,
But long before the month was up,
  The loving cup was broken.
      Fala, fala!
But long before the month was up,
  The loving cup was broken.'

'What do you want to sing that stuff for?' said the baker's wife. ''Taint sense.'

'I can't understand it,' said Frances, 'but it's nice. Isn't there any more?'

'It *is* silly,' said Monday, 'but you sing it nicely, so do go on.'

'There's a lot more of it,' said the baker, 'but I can't think of the words. So now, my dears, if you want any more, you must sing for yourselves.'

So they all sang the songs they had learnt at school, and the evening, which had started with quarrelling, ended happily for everyone.

After that, Monday did not cause quite so much trouble for a time. She still refused to go to school. Nor did the baker's wife want to let her help in the house, because she broke things and got in the way. One day she was followed into the house by a little scraggy grey cat with only one ear. The cat would not leave her, so it had to be adopted. It was a good mouser, but it was not a very clean cat as most cats are, and the baker's wife did not like it. All the same, the children were fond of it, for it would rub itself against their legs and tickle them. It sometimes scratched, and then the baker's wife would get angry and try to throw it out. But either the children stuck up for it, or else it was put out of the door and returned again as soon as possible, so that the baker's wife gave up trying to get rid of it.

Little Monday did not stay good for very long. If the baker's wife put clean clothes on her, they were sure to be torn and dirty before the day was out. If the baker left his spectacles and his books on a shelf beside the fire, Monday upset them for him and lost his place. Tom's toys would be left out in the rain and Frances' dolls soon began to look untidy and dirty as Monday herself. She was a hopeless child, perfectly hopeless. It seemed as if nothing could be done about her. Yet she was never really sorry. She simply enjoyed being a nuisance. She laughed as if all her teeth would fly out when her grey cat tangled up the baker's wife's knitting when she was in the middle of making a winter vest for the baby that had been born next door.

The baker's wife talked a lot more over the garden wall than she had used to, and now it was always about little Monday that she talked. She told the neighbours what a terrible trial the child was and what a lot of bother she caused. The neighbours asked why she didn't try to send Monday to a home for naughty children, but the baker's wife said she didn't feel like doing that, and besides, she did not know how to set about it. So things went on as before. It seemed as if little Monday had come to stay for ever, and as if she would never get any better and always be a terrible trial and a bother.

One evening things were worse than usual. The whole family had been annoyed by little Monday. She was now sitting in the middle of the floor stroking her ugly grey cat. Tom was doing his lessons, Frances was reading a book, the baker's wife was polishing a pair of candlesticks, and the baker was trying to mend the side of his glasses which Monday had broken.

'She's a dratted nuisance,' he said. 'How can I read my newspaper with my specs all a-broken; that's what I'm asking?'

'It's no great matter for that,' said his wife. 'There's never anything in the paper – I've often heard you say so. But where am I going to find breakfast for us all when she's broken every egg that I bought from the grocer only yesterday?'

'And why did she go and leave my new pram out in the garden, so that the rain has spoilt it?' said poor Frances.

'And why do you go messing about with my books when I'm not looking and leaving marks on the pages?' asked Tom.

But little Monday said nothing, and only sat and fondled her one-eared cat. All the same, she was not laughing. She was looking thoughtful and rather sad.

'What have we all done to be troubled so by a worthless, good-for-naught, bothersome urchin that is no good to nobody?' said the baker. 'It's not as if we were evil folk like the Philistines or Pharaoh of Egypt, to be troubled with all the twelve plagues rolled into one. We're good folk, we are – hard-working and as honest as most. What have we done to deserve *you*, I should like to know?'

But little Monday looked at him thoughtfully, and all she said was:

'There's no sense in plaguing *wicked* people. They make enough trouble for themselves.'

'Why plague *anybody*?' asked the baker's wife crossly. 'Isn't there trouble enough in the world without making more?'

Monday sighed.

'I can't help it,' she said. 'I just can't help it, Besides, I do love it so.'

Everybody made angry noises and went out of the room – everyone except Frances, who went on reading her book.

Monday went across to Frances and put her arms round her and began crying.

'You don't like me, Francie, do you? You all hate me.'

'We like you all right really,' said Frances. 'Only why do you do such naughty things? You needn't have left my pram out in the garden. And why did you go and put mud on my lovely new pinafore?'

'I couldn't help it,' said Monday. 'Pinafores are such silly things. It looked so funny on you – all clean and white and covered with silly lambs and things.'

'Lambs *aren't* silly,' said Frances.

'Anyway, if you loved me, you wouldn't mind a bit of mud on your pinny. Your mother can wash it off. She likes washing.'

'She doesn't,' said Frances.

'Well, why does she do so much of it then? You hate me, all of you. That's all about it.'

And once more she began to cry. Frances saw that it was no use arguing with her, so she went on reading her book.

After tea little Monday was nowhere to be found. Nor was the grey cat to be seen. Nobody bothered. They were probably out together doing mischief somewhere, and it was a relief not to have them in the house. They all settled peacefully down to their tasks till it was nearly time for bed. Everyone pretended not to care where Monday was, but privately they were all a little worried. The weather outside was rather horrid. It was not exactly raining, but there was a damp gusty wind, and the baker said he thought it would be a stormy night.

Then suddenly he sniffed and got up from his chair.

'What's that smell?' he said.

They all sniffed.

'Smells like burning to me,' said the baker's wife. 'Now what did I leave in the oven?'

But the smell was not coming from the oven, it was coming from outside.

The baker went towards the outer door, but it was flung open in his face, and the untidy figure of little Monday appeared on the threshold in a gust of showery wind.

'Better look out!' she cried. 'The bakehouse is burning!'

'You young demon!' shouted the baker. 'What have you been up to now?'

Monday did indeed look like a demon. Her hair was partly burnt away and her face was blackened and bleeding. Her clothes were torn. A sleeve had been ripped quite away and one of her stockings was down to her ankle. Water dripped from what was left of her clothes.

She began to laugh. The baker made a grab for her, but she

rushed out into the yard towards the burning bakehouse. The baker followed her. His wife and the children quickly put coats on and went after him.

The flames were rushing upwards and great clouds of black smoke were blown here, there and everywhere by the wind. There was not enough rain to quench the fire. There was a crackling of burning timber. Little Monday was running to and fro, staggering under the weight of a bucket of water, constantly refilled from a barrel in the yard, which she threw on to the flames. The baker and the others ran for more buckets; and, choked with smoke, they poured them upon the fire from as near as they could approach. Presently some neighbours came and lent a hand, and someone ran for the fire brigade. But it was hopeless. The fire became fiercer and fiercer. Soon they could not get near enough to reach the flames with buckets of water. They had to stand back and watch the bakehouse burn. Frances was crying beside her mother. Suddenly Tom said:

'Where's Monday?'

The little girl was found lying in the ground near the empty water barrel, choking and gasping with smoke and exhaustion. The baker carried her indoors, took her upstairs, and laid her on the bed.

'What did you do it for?' said the baker sadly. 'Whatever did you set my bakehouse afire for?'

He gave her some water, and she tried to sit up but sank back again. Then she said feebly:

'I didn't, truly I didn't. It wasn't me, I tell you.'

Then she fainted, and the baker's wife covered her with the bedclothes to keep her warm, first taking off her wet things. The others came upstairs and stood beside the bed.

In the morning the bakehouse was found to be quite burnt down. It was still smoking and smouldering, but little of it was left standing. The fire brigade had come too late.

Monday was better, but still very feeble. Between gasps and coughs she told them what had happened. She had been for a walk, and as she came back towards evening she had heard two men talking. She had hidden and listened. At first she could not hear what they said. Then she heard that they were going to set something on fire. How surprised she was when she heard that it was nothing else than the baker's bakehouse. They muttered something about the price of bread, and how it was too high, and people couldn't pay so much for their bread. This would teach them, they said. This would make them think. Monday did not understand all this, but she knew there was going to be trouble, and she liked trouble. Where there was trouble, there would she be. She followed the men carefully so as not to be seen. She thought of running on and telling the baker, but she did not see how she could pass them without being seen. They sneaked into the bakehouse, and Monday went in after them. One of them was carrying a tin of something. He splashed it about, spreading it as fast as he could over the floor and walls. He emptied the last of it on to a pile of old flour sacks. Then the other one said, 'That'll do,' and took out a box of matches. He struck one of them and threw it into the flour sacks. Then, when the sacks began to flare up, the first man said 'Come on!' and both of them ran out of the building. That was the last Monday saw of them. She had been hiding behind the oven so that they should not see her. The flour sacks were behind the door, and Monday only got out with the greatest difficulty. She was not at all frightened, because she enjoyed trouble. She knew just what to do. Seizing the pail that always stood beside the water barrel in a corner of the yard, she filled it and ran back into the bakehouse. She threw it on the flames and went for more. She did this several times, until she began to feel tired. The fire kept breaking out in different places. When she knew she couldn't put it out she had gone to the house and told the baker.

When her story was finished, Monday lay back in the bed and closed her eyes. Nobody said anything.

'What a story!' thought the baker's wife to herself. 'Wonder where those two men came from. Did it herself and was too frightened to say.'

Everyone went out of the room except Frances. Monday sat up and said:

'They don't believe me, do they? None of you believe me.'

Frances said nothing and followed the others out of the room. For the rest of the day they nursed little Monday and she became strong again, but nobody said much to her. She had fought bravely against the fire, but everyone thought she had started it. Nobody believed the story of the two men and the tin of oil.

Next morning, when the baker's wife went in to see Monday, she had gone. The bed was untidy, and some of Frances' clothes were missing. Monday was nowhere to be found.

'Oh well,' said the baker's wife. 'She'll turn up like a bad ha'penny, when she's least expected. Meanwhile, there's one less breakfast to cook.'

But Monday didn't turn up. Instead, half-way through the morning, two policemen came on bicycles. They told the baker that two rough-looking men had been caught the night before trying to burn down another bakery in a town some ten miles away. So it looked as if little Monday's story was true after all. Yes, said the policemen, they had owned up to trying to burn down the baker's bakehouse the night before that. Now the baker and his family began to be sorry that Monday had gone. She had been a naughty little troublemaker, but she had evidently not done so dreadful a thing as burn down a house. They questioned the police about her, but nothing was known. The police promised to look out for her and make inquiries.

Days and weeks passed, but still Monday did not come back. The bakehouse was rebuilt out of the money that the baker had saved, and after a few months they had all settled down peacefully, and life was much the same as it had been before they had ever set eyes on Monday. The new bakehouse was better and more up-to-date than the old one had been, and soon the baker was doing well and making up for the business he had lost during the weeks when he had been able to do no baking.

Tom got to the top of his class, and Frances kept her dolls as neat and tidy as ever. Their mother went on with her sewing and cooking and cleaning, and never made any more unkind remarks about the baker's pipe.

But something was missing. They could never be quite as happy as they had been in the days before little Monday had come and dripped on the hearthrug. The neighbours did not gossip over the wall with the baker's wife, because there was not so much to gossip about. There was no Monday to grumble at, for the stories of her misdeeds had always been something to talk about. True, there were fewer cups broken, and fewer balls of wool were tangled up, and Tom's toys were not left out at night and Frances' pinafore was not covered with mud. All the same, something was missing.

'It's not the same without her,' said Frances.

'It certainly isn't,' said Tom. 'No more broken dolls.'

'No more singing,' said Frances.

'That's right,' said Tom. 'I used to like the singing. I wonder why father doesn't sing now.'

'She was rather horrid, you know.'

'Yes. All the same, I sometimes wish she was back.'

Then one Sunday they all went out to tea with an aunt who lived several streets away. When they came back, it was dark. The baker went to the table in the middle of the room where the lamp always stood. As he felt in his pocket for matches, he heard a faint purring sound. He lit the lamp. When the flame had burnt up, he saw, sitting on the table, an ugly grey cat with one ear. It bounded down from the table and rubbed itself against his leg.

'Hello,' said the baker, 'where have I seen you before?'

'Hello,' said his wife, 'who's been at my knitting? I'm sure I left it tidy when we went out.'

'Hello,' said Tom, 'who's been using my paint-box and got all the colours mixed up?'

'Hello,' said Frances, 'where's my best doll gone? I'm sure I left her sitting in the armchair.'

'Somebody's been here,' said the baker's wife. 'I told you we ought to have locked the front door.'

'It's that girl,' said the baker. 'And I did lock the front door. She'd get in anywhere, that young scallywag.'

But Monday was nowhere to be found. They looked in the kitchen and the yard and the bakehouse, and there was not a sign of her. The baker's wife took a candle and went upstairs to put away her best coat and hat. A moment later she came to the top of the stairs and said:

'Come upstairs, all of you, and bring the lamp. I've something to show you.'

They all went up to the big bedroom. There fast asleep in the middle of the bed, and tucked up in the clean eiderdown, was a ragged, grubby little girl with black hair and a wide grinning mouth. Clutched in her grimy arms was Frances' best doll.

The baker and his wife and Tom and Frances stood round the bed in silence, not daring to wake her.

'I wonder if she's come for always this time,' said Frances.

The baker's wife sighed and turned to her husband.

'I wish she could sleep like that all the time,' she said, 'even in my best eiderdown.'

Then the little girl in bed turned in her sleep and smiled, showing all her teeth.

'Come on, children,' said the baker quietly. 'Best come downstairs and get supper.'

'And hurry off to bed,' said their mother. 'Monday tomorrow.'

Poor Fish

A doctor was sitting at dinner one day when his servant came in and told him that a poor villager had come with a cart full of wood. He had unloaded it in the shed at the end of the yard, and was now waiting to be paid.

'Send him in,' ordered the doctor, and the poor carter, removing his hat, stepped into the dining-room.

'How much do I owe you?' asked the doctor.

'One guinea, if you please, sir,' answered the man.

The doctor gave him the money and then poured out a glass of wine.

'Here,' he said, 'you look thirsty. Drink this.'

The man took the wine gladly, and when he had drunk it, he stood looking at the doctor as he sat at dinner.

How fine to be a doctor and live like this, he thought. I wonder if I could learn to be a doctor.

So he told the doctor what was in his mind, and the doctor said 'I'll tell you what to do. First, sell your horse and cart, and buy a black gown and wig like mine. Next, have a plate with your name printed on it to hang up outside your door. What *is* your name?'

'My name is Fish,' said the poor man.

'That will never do,' said the doctor. 'You must call yourself "Doctor Knowall". Have that name painted on a sign. You'll find people will come along fast enough.'

So poor Fish thanked the doctor and went off and did as he had been told. He sold his horse and cart and bought a doctor's gown and wig. Then he had a sign hung up outside his house saying:

DOCTOR KNOWALL

Everyone who came that way thought he must be a very wise man indeed.

He had not long set up as a doctor before a splendid coach stopped at his door. It had a coat of arms in gold letters on the side of it, for it belonged to a rich Count. Out of the coach stepped the Count's steward.

'If you are the great Doctor Knowall,' he said, 'get into this coach, for the Count wants you to have dinner with him. He lost a large sum of money and it is believed to be stolen. He commands you to find out who stole it. He thinks it is one of the servants, but he has so many that he can't tell which is the thief. Hurry up, for my master is waiting.'

Now Fish had a wife called Meg, and when she heard where her husband was going, she decided to go with him. She too wanted to dine at the Count's table and to look at his palace. So Fish told the steward he would come if he might bring his wife.

'Very good,' said the steward, 'only hurry, for my master is very anxious to know who the thief is.'

On the way Meg asked her husband what the palace would be like.

'How should I know?' answered Fish. 'One thing is certain, though: there will be a great many servants. I shouldn't wonder if there are three or four of them to serve dinner.'

'Get along with you,' answered Meg. 'I don't believe a word of it.'

'Well, we shall see,' answered Fish.

Before long they reached the Count's palace, and at once they were made to sit down with the Count at his table, and dinner was served. Now the money had indeed been stolen, not by one of the servants but by several. They had taken it, and hidden it under a stone in the yard, meaning to share it among themselves as soon as they got the chance. One of the thieves had been told by the Count's coachman that a great doctor, a very wise man who knew everything, had been sent for to discover who had stolen the money. So they were very nervous.

Well, the meal was begun, and as the fish dish was brought in by one of the servants, Fish turned to his wife and said 'There! That's the first of them.'

Of course he only meant that it was the first of the servants he had told her about in the coach; but the servant overheard him and thought he meant 'the first of the thieves'. This upset him very badly, for he was indeed one of those who had stolen the money.

He went out and told his fellows, so that when it was the second one's turn to bring in a dish, this servant didn't want to go in. But they made him, and when he set down his dish on the table, Fish said to Meg, 'And that's the second of them.'

The second servant was sure that the great Doctor Knowall had guessed the truth, and when he told his fellows what had been said, the third servant was even more unwilling to enter the dining-hall. You can imagine his terror when, as soon as he set down his dish upon the table, Fish turned to his wife and muttered 'There you are, my dear, that's the third of them!'

When the fourth servant came in with a covered dish, the Count turned to Doctor Knowall and said 'After dinner, Doctor, I shall ask you to tell me who has stolen my money. But first let us see how clever you are. Since you know everything, tell me what is under that silver dish-cover.'

The poor man had not the slightest idea. How was he to guess what was under the cover? So thinking he would be ruined, he could not help saying to his wife, 'Alas, poor Fish!'

The Count ordered the servant to raise the cover, and there – sure enough – lay a fine fish, steaming in rich sauce.

'Congratulations, Doctor Knowall!' said the Count. 'Now I am sure you'll be able to tell me what I want to know.'

When the fourth servant got back to the kitchen where the other thieves waited, he was trembling with fright.

'He knows everything,' said the servant. 'We had better have a word with him, and try to stop him giving us away.'

So one of them went to the door of the dining-hall and signed to Doctor Knowall to come and have a word with them. They told

him that, if he would promise not to give them away, they would
show him where the money was hidden. They would give him a
reward out of their own savings, but if he told the Count who they
were, they would all be hanged and the Doctor would not get so
great a reward. Fish agreed to do what they asked, so they showed
him the stone in the yard where the money was hidden.

After dinner Fish told the Count that he wasn't able to name
the thieves, but he could tell him where to find his money. The
Count then followed him into the yard, and under the stone they
found nearly all the missing money. He was so grateful that he
gave Fish a handsome reward, thanked him, and bade him good-
bye. Then the thieving servants also gave him money for not
having given them away. So Fish and his wife Meg went back
home well satisfied and, with all the money they had been given,
managed to live for a long while in ease and comfort.

Sir Gammar Vance

Last Sunday morning at six o'clock in the evening, as I was sailing over the tops of the mountains in my little boat, I met two men on horseback riding on one mare: so I asked them, 'Could they tell me whether the little old woman was dead yet who was hanged last Saturday week for drowning herself in a shower of feathers?'

They said they could not positively inform me, but if I went to Sir Gammer Vance, he could tell me all about it.

'But how am I to know the house?' said I.

'Ho, 'tis easy enough,' they said, 'for 'tis a brick house, built entirely of flints, standing alone by itself in the middle of sixty or seventy others just like it.'

'Oh, nothing in the world is easier,' said I.

'Nothing *can* be easier,' they said: so I went on my way.

Now this Sir Gammer Vance was a giant, and a bottle-maker. And like all giants who are also bottle-makers, he lived in a little thumb-bottle just outside his own front door.

'How d'ye do?' says he.

'Very well, I thank you,' says I.

'Have some breakfast with me?'

'With all my heart,' says I.

So he gave me a slice of beer, and a cup of cold veal; and there was a little dog under the table that picked up all the crumbs. 'Hang him,' says I.

'No, don't hang him,' says he: 'for he killed a hare yesterday, and if you don't believe me, I'll show you the hare alive in a basket.'

So he took me into his garden to show me the curiosities. In one corner there was a fox hatching eagle's eggs; in another there was an iron apple tree, entirely covered with pears and lead; in the third there was the hare which the dog had killed yesterday, alive in the basket; and in the fourth there were twenty-four hipper switches threshing tobacco, and at the sight of me they threshed so hard that they drove the plug through the wall, and through a little dog that was passing by on the other side.

I, hearing the dog howl, jumped over the wall; and turned it as neatly inside out as possible, when it ran away as if it had not an hour to live.

Then he took me into the park to show me his deer: and I remembered that I had a warrant in my pocket to shoot venison for His Majesty's dinner. So I set fire to my bow, poised my arrow, and shot amongst them. I broke seventeen ribs on one side, and twenty-one and a half on the other; but my arrow passed clean through without ever touching it, and the worst was, I lost my arrow: however, I found it again in the hollow of a tree. I felt it; it felt clammy. I smelt it, it smelt honey.

'Huzza!' said I, 'a wild bee's nest,' when out sprang a covey of partridges. I shot at them; some say I killed eighteen; but I am sure I killed thirty-six besides a dead salmon which was flying over the bridge, of which I made the best apple pie I ever tasted.

Sailor Rumbelow
and Britannia

'I'm lonesome,' said Dick to himself, standing on the deck of the three-masted schooner. 'I'll whistle to keep up my spirits.'

For the twenty-third time that day he whistled to himself a gay hornpipe tune. But it didn't cheer him up.

He had been standing just there, on the deck of the schooner, with his telescope to his eye, for nearly as long as he could remember. His first name was Dick, and he had a fine roaring surname, which was Rumbelow. The sails of his schooner were spread tight in the wind, just as they always were. But there was no wind. There was no one else in sight. The captain and the mate and the rest of the crew must be down below somewhere. Dick Rumbelow felt lonely, cold and small. The tune he was whistling did nothing to make him feel warm and big, as a sailor should. He could not even dance a hornpipe to make himself warm.

Now this was not surprising, for Dick was only about a quarter of an inch high, about as high as a dried pea or a little boy's front tooth. Of course he didn't know this; and he didn't know that he was on the deck of a model ship in full sail, inside a glass bottle. From inside the bottle he couldn't see the bottle, so how was he to know that he was inside it? All the same, Sailor Rumbelow had an idea that his ship, the *Desperado* – that was what it was called – was becalmed. The sails might bulge stiffly, and the painted blue waves have white crests; but still he could feel no breeze, and no movement. So all day long Dick stood on the deck, sometimes whistling and sometimes thinking about the times he could almost remember before the *Desperado* was becalmed. He had a notion about long, exciting voyages to palmy shores and fights with black men who shouted terrible war-cries and rattled their spears and shields.

One day a lady with a little girl came into the shop where the *Desperado*, inside its bottle, hung in the window. The shopkeeper came out and asked what she wanted. While the lady was talking to the shopkeeper, the little girl stared at the ship in the bottle. She couldn't take her eyes off it. She pulled at her mother's hand.

'Look, mummy,' she said, 'oh, look!'

'Don't interrupt, dear,' said the lady.

But at last she stopped talking to the shopkeeper and turned to her daughter.

'It's a little ship, mummy. It's in a bottle. How did it get in the bottle with its masts and sails all sticking up?'

The shopkeeper explained that the ship had probably been made by a sailor, perhaps a hundred years ago, and put inside the bottle with its sails and masts lying on the deck. Then he must have pulled them up into position and fastened them there before pushing the cork into the bottle-neck.

'It's lovely,' said the little girl. 'Can we buy it, mummy?'

'It's not a toy, dear,' said her mother. 'If you played with it, you could so easily break it.'

'Oh, I wouldn't play with it. I'd just look at it. We could hang it in the window.'

'Well, I'll see what daddy says,' answered the lady.

The little girl knew that this often meant that something she wanted would be bought. She squeezed her mother's hand in gratitude, as if it was all settled, and they went out of the shop.

Next day they came in again and bought the schooner *Desperado*, inside its bottle, with Dick Rumbelow standing on the deck, his telescope to his eye.

When the bottle was hung up in the window of the lady's house just outside the town, Dick could see across a green lawn to a huge sea, and this made him happier. Of course the huge sea was only a lily-pond, but to Dick it was as big as the Caribbean.

'Yo ho!' he said in his most seamanlike voice. 'This is something like.'

*

In a little red-brick house, inside a glass ball, lived a very tiny girl. Her name was Britannia. Although she was so very tiny, she was grown up – about twenty years old, you would have said, looking at her pretty golden hair and her red cheeks. Yet she was no taller than a small dried pea or the front tooth of a real little girl. Her house was only a finger's height, and the two green bushes at either side of the front door were very small indeed. There was a neat green lawn that went all round the house, but it was nearly always covered with snow. So was the roof of the red-brick house. Britannia always stood just inside one of the top windows, looking out over the snowy lawn. When you lifted up the glass ball with the house inside, and turned it upside down, then the right way up again, there was a tremendous snowstorm. You couldn't see the house, or Britannia, or the two green bushes, or the green lawn, because of the whirling snowflakes. Round and round they went, until very slowly they settled just as before, covering the roof and the lawn and the green bushes on either side of the front door.

Snowstorms always caused Britannia much trouble and inconvenience, because they meant that the house was turned upside down; all her pots and pans and tables and chairs and teacups and vases and everything else in her small, tidy house went flying up to the ceiling; and when they came down, she had to put them all to rights again, while the snowflakes whirled about outside the windows. But before the snow had settled, she was back again at her old place just inside one of the top windows, gazing out over the white world. Her cheeks were always red and shiny because of the bother of clearing everything up, and her golden hair was never quite tidy. It smudged down over her eyes; and this was a pity because she was one who liked to be tidy.

One day the little girl and her mother came into the shop once more, and the little girl saw the house in the snow. It was on the shelf just inside the shop window. While her mother was talking to the shopkeeper, the little girl picked up the glass ball and looked at it.

'Careful, dear,' her mother said.

Then the shopkeeper showed her how to make it snow. She almost cried with delight.

'We really can't afford it,' said her mother. 'Why, it's no time since we bought the *Desperado*.'

The little girl looked at her mother wide-eyed.

'You're not *sorry* we bought it, mummy?' she asked. 'Everybody says how lovely it is.'

'No, of course not, but we can't have everything.'

'Wouldn't this look lovely in the same room as the ship?' said the little girl. 'A ship in a bottle and a house in a ball – what could be nicer?'

'We'll see what daddy says.'

'Oh yes, let's.'

'Mind you, I'm not promising anything.'

'No, of course not.'

But the little girl had an idea that her father might buy the house in the snowstorm.

'I must say,' said her father to her mother that evening, 'the child has good taste.'

The little girl, who was listening, could not understand this. She often couldn't quite understand daddy. How could he know she had a good taste if he had never tasted her? Still, it was said in a pleased way, you could tell that; and that was all that mattered.

'I expect she takes after you, dear,' said the lady artfully.

'Oh well –' said the little girl's father in a voice which meant he would almost certainly do what she wanted.

When they bought the house in the snow it looked beautiful on the mantelpiece. The little girl was told to be very careful and not play with it unless there was someone with her to see that she didn't accidentally drop it. She loved being allowed to take it in her hands and turn it first upside down, then right side up, so that the little red-brick house was almost lost in a whirl of snowflakes.

For the first few days after her removal, Britannia seemed to be always tidying up; but after a while she was left more to herself. Then she began to enjoy her new situation. Certainly the room was very elegant to look at. Sometimes the glass ball, after being very carefully dusted by the lady herself, was put back a little crooked, so that Britannia could see the window and the garden beyond. She could see the *Desperado* in its glass bottle hanging in the window, and she could just make out Dick Rumbelow standing on the deck with his spyglass to his eye.

'What a nice fellow he looks,' she said to herself, 'and how lonely. Poor man! I wonder how he likes living in a bottle. It must seem awfully cramped to one used to voyaging on the foaming seas.'

The lady also took down the ship in the bottle once a week and dusted it. She never let anyone else do this, for fear it might fall and break. Sometimes she put it back the wrong way round, so that Sailor Dick no longer looked out of the window at the Caribbean lily-pond but right across the room towards the mantelpiece. So it was that he first set eyes on Britannia as she stood by the top window in her house in the snow.

He gazed long and silently at her through his spyglass. He was afraid she might think him rude but he just couldn't help it.

'My eye!' said Dick. 'What a beautiful girl! I've never seen such bright rosy cheeks and golden hair in all my life. I dare say her cheeks are red from being out in the snow. But how lonely she must be, living in a glass ball like that. Poor girl, what a cold and lonesome life!'

But Britannia did not at all mind being stared at through the telescope. It had never happened to her before, and she liked it.

'Let him stare,' she said. 'I will not wave at him, though I should like to, but I won't look angry either. He must be so lonely inside that bottle, and if staring at me through a telescope cheers him up, who am I to forbid it?'

For a whole week Sailor Rumbelow looked hard at the girl in the red-brick house. He could not take his eyes off her.

'She doesn't seem to mind,' he said to himself. 'I even fancy she may be pleased. It looks as if she's all alone in that great house. She never comes out and nobody visits her. I suppose they don't like the snow. Well, I can't blame them. But it must be lonely for the girl up there. If she likes my company through the wrong end of a spyglass, so to say, it'd be cruel to deny her.'

Then at the end of the week the lady came and dusted the things in the room; Britannia was made to look away from the window, but Dick was left as he had been, staring at the house in the snow as it stood on the mantelpiece.

'Now I've gone and offended her,' said the sailor to himself. 'She doesn't look at me any more. Poor soul, all by herself in that glass ball! If only I could sail alongside of her and break in! Then perhaps we two could go walking out together, like – like –'

But he couldn't remember walking out with any girl, even though he knew he had once, long ago, been on shore. Still, sailors nearly always walk out with girls when they are on shore, so Dick supposed there must have been someone.

'All the same,' he said to himself, 'if there *was* someone, she couldn't have been a patch on the one with the red cheeks and the gold ringlets.'

And he sighed for Britannia all the more because she had turned away from him and would not be stared at any longer.

'She's angry with me,' Dick told himself, 'because she wants rescuing, and I can't rescue her. That's what it is. Shut away in that house like that, with the snow all round: what she wants is rescuing – or perhaps she wants a smell of the salt sea! Ah, if only the wind would blow, and I could fetch up right alongside.'

Next week it was the other way round. When the lady came to dust, whisking round with her little feather brush and her yellow duster, she left Dick Rumbelow staring out of the window and Britannia gazing towards him.

'He's lost interest in me,' sighed Britannia to herself. 'Just because I couldn't see him for a whole week, he's got tired of me and won't look any more. That's so like a sailor. You never can trust them. All the same, I won't give him up. He needs me, poor chap, shut up in that glass bottle, and I won't desert him.'

So she sighed for Dick, and Dick sighed for her as he gazed out over the Caribbean. Outside, the days grew warmer and sunnier, but inside the glass ball the snow lay on the ground as thick as ever. Sometimes the window was left open, and this made a little breeze in the room, and the ship in the bottle moved ever so slightly on the cords by which it hung from the ceiling. And Dick Rumbelow fancied the wind was getting up, and soon he would be able to turn the good ship *Desperado* and bring her to where he might rescue the girl in the glass ball. He whistled the tune of 'The Girl I Left Behind Me', and after that his favourite hornpipe, but still the ship did not move, although the sails were as stiff and bulging as ever. But the week passed, and once more Dick and Britannia were facing each other.

'He has forgiven me,' said the girl to herself happily. 'Now surely I can wave and smile at him, because we are friends again.'

'So she's not angry with me after all,' said Dick to himself, 'and I will dance a hornpipe and wave my spyglass to show my regard for her.'

Then he saw that Britannia seemed to be smiling and waving

to him, and Britannia noticed that her sailor friend looked as if
he was actually doing a hornpipe to amuse her. So she smiled and
waved all the more prettily, and Dick waved his spyglass in the
air and shouted 'Huzza!'

Of course, all this time the little girl who had got her mother
and father to buy the ship and the little house in the snow had been
coming to the room to look at them and play with them when she
was allowed to. The sailor and the tiny person in the house had
got used to this. Then she did not come any more. At first they
were so glad to be looking at one another and smiling and waving
that they did not notice it. Then after a while they wondered why
they were left so much alone. The reason was this. The little girl
was ill. She had gone to a party and caught the whooping-cough.
She had been made to stay in bed in her own room and could not
come downstairs. Except for the coughing she was not unhappy.
She had toys and books with her in bed, and the Dutch girl who
lived in the house and helped the lady used to come and talk to
her and play with her. At last the little girl was allowed out of bed

in her dressing-gown, but still she had to stay in her own room, which was warm and sunny.

'Judy,' she said one day to the Dutch girl. 'Judy dear, will you do something for me? Go downstairs and fetch the ship in the bottle. I want to look at it again. I haven't seen it for ages.'

'I don't think I ought to,' said the Dutch girl. 'Mummy wouldn't like it.'

'Oh, please, Judy,' begged the little girl, 'just this once. I'd be terribly careful.'

'Well, we'll see,' said the Dutch girl.

After tea the little girl sat on the bed holding the ship in the bottle. There it was, just as it had been all those ages before she had got the whooping-cough. There was the sailor with his telescope; there were the three sloping masts and the stiff white sails.

'Judy,' said the little girl, 'do *one* more thing for me, will you? Fetch me the little house in the snow. Just this once. Oh, please!'

The Dutch girl did as she was asked. Everybody did what the little girl asked, sooner or later. People said she was spoilt, but it couldn't be helped because she was lonely. And she was always so pleased and grateful.

'Oh, thank you, dear Judy,' she said when the Dutch girl brought her the house in the snow.

'Now mind,' said Judy, 'only for five minutes. Then it's time for a bath.'

She went to turn on the bath, while the little girl made a snowstorm in the glass ball. She held it very, very carefully, for it would be terrible if it fell and broke. Then Judy called her to her bath, and she put the ball down gently on the floor, near where the bottle lay on its side on the window-sill. Then she did up the cord of her dressing-gown tighter, and ran off to the bathroom.

The *Desperado*, inside its bottle on the window-sill, lay on its side. Dick Rumbelow, still fixed firmly to the deck, was just able to see over the edge of the window-sill. With his telescope he could make out the glass ball, which stood on the floor beneath. He couldn't quite see Britannia, but he could see the roof of her house, with the last snowflakes just settling quietly upon it. He knew that Britannia was inside the house, perhaps wondering what had become of her sailor friend. For she could certainly not see him.

'Well,' said Dick to himself, trembling all over with excitement, 'it's now or never. That girl needs rescuing. If ever a girl needed rescuing, it's that girl in the snow. Here goes!'

So he rocked himself to and fro on the deck, and thought about all the storms he had ever seen or heard of, and a good many that he hadn't. The window was open, and a pleasant evening breeze began to flap the curtains this way and that. Soon Dick fancied he could hear the thunder rumbling in the distance and catch sight of an occasional flash of lightning.

Britannia, in the little red house in the snow, could hear nothing of this. She was anxious about Dick, whom she couldn't see, and she did not like being on the floor. There was no view except the dark space under the bed; she began to feel afraid, and called upon her sailor.

'Oh, sailor boy,' she said, wringing her hands, 'if only you were here. It's getting dark, and I'm terribly lonely. What's happened to you? Perhaps you're out in a storm. Perhaps you'll be drowned, and I shall never see you again!'

Dick could not hear her, but he imagined he heard her calling.

'I'm coming,' he cried. 'Keep your spirits up, my girl, and I'll be alongside in two flicks of a mermaid's tail!'

Then he made a mighty plunge, and the curtain gave an extra flap, and in two flicks of a mermaid's tail the bottle had rolled to the edge of the window-sill and toppled over.

It missed the glass ball by half an inch, but the bottle was smashed. The ship lay on its side on the floor, one of the masts split in two, and the pieces of glass were scattered all round.

Dick picked himself up. He was no longer on the deck of the *Desperado*. He felt very shaken.

'Thunder and lightning!' he cried. 'It's the French! There's been nothing like this since Trafalgar. No, it's not the French – it's the almightiest howling tempest that hit the fleet. Where's the girl in the snow?'

Then he saw that he was looking right into Britannia's red-brick house. He had never been so near her before. He was close up against the glass ball. The snow was so near, he could have put out his hand and touched it if it hadn't been for the glass. There was the lawn, and the two green bushes, the front door, and the window where Britannia gazed out at him. Yes, there she was, anxious but smiling, the golden hair smudged over her eyes and her red cheeks shining like two apples. Then Dick reached for his telescope, which had fallen from his hand, and began to beat it against the side of the glass ball, just above his head.

Britannia watched him, not moving.

'So he came at last,' she sighed. 'Brave fellow! He's broken out of his bottle, and faced the storm and the snow, all to visit me. Soon he'll be knocking at the door, and I shall let him in and take him by the hands. And it won't matter a bit that he'll have snow on his boots. I'll never let him go, and there'll be plenty of time to clear up the mess.'

Dick was still banging on the glass with his telescope. He was beginning to feel terribly tired after his fall.

'Come and lend a hand!' he called. 'Bring a hammer or something.'

But Britannia could not hear him.

'Whatever is he doing, waving his spyglass like that? Why doesn't he come up the path? What's stopping him?'

Then she saw that her sailor had given up trying to reach her, and had dropped exhausted to the ground. At last she understood that she too lived inside glass. She had thought that only the sailor was shut in, but now she knew that her own little house in the snow was surrounded by a transparent wall that she could never break. She stared out of the window at the broken pieces of bottle, the wrecked schooner, and Sailor Dick Rumbelow lying on the ground not twenty yards from her own front door. After that, she knew nothing.

The house in the snow was never again left on the mantelpiece. It was kept for safety in a cabinet with a big glass door, so that it could be seen and not touched. The lady had at first been very angry, but Judy and the little girl had cried such a lot that she had to forgive them. Each said it was all her own fault. The tiny sailor was picked up, but his telescope was never found. The ship was mended, and once again Dick was fixed to the deck. The broken mast was repaired. Then the little girl's father took it back to the shop, and the shopkeeper got a very clever man, an old sailor who sometimes did odd jobs for him, to put it safely in a new bottle. So there was the *Desperado* a little scratched, not quite as smart as it had been before, but almost as beautiful. The fall had not damaged it badly.

'Don't let's hang it in the window any more, mummy,' said the little girl. 'You never know. It might be blown down, or the string might break, or somebody knock it with a broom. Don't let's ever break it any more.'

'Where shall we put it, dear?' asked the lady.

'Beside the house in the snow, of course,' answered the little girl. 'That's much the safest place.'

So, instead of the cord, a neat wooden stand was made, and

the bottle stood just beside the ball in the glass cabinet. And Dick, who no longer had his spyglass, and Britannia with her red cheeks and golden hair, once more looked at each other quite close to. This went on day after day, except sometimes, very occasionally, when it was the little girl's birthday, or an important visitor called. Then the good ship *Desperado*, with one of its masts a little bent, would be taken out and admired; and the house in the glass ball would be turned upside down and back again, to set the snow dancing madly about, while all the pots and pans and cups and saucers inside the house were tumbled about in confusion. Then Britannia would sigh and start putting them to rights again, just as she always did.

'After all,' she said to herself, 'my very near neighbour, my sailor friend, *might* drop in to see me one day, and I should hate the house to be in a pickle if *that* happened.'

Foo the Potter

Long ago, in the land of Chen, which is far away in the eastern half of the world, there lived a Princess called Lo-Yen. She was young, beautiful, and passionately fond of music. Now in those days – so long ago it was – the people of Chen did not have music like ours, music on instruments and on bells, and the music of voices. They did not have tunes made up of a series of notes, now high, now low, now soft and now loud. No, their music was made on vases, and each tune consisted of one note only, or at most two or three, made by tapping the side of a vase with a little hammer. The hammer was a wooden ball on the end of a short bamboo stick, and the ball was covered with a piece of kid-skin, so that it did not crack the vase.

It was the object of all the potters in the land of Chen to make a vase more beautiful and of a purer tone than any that had been made before. Each year, in the fifth month, all the makers of vases throughout the land would go up to the palace of the Princess Lo-Yen and take their vases. There was a solemn contest or competition, and the maker of the most beautiful vase would be rewarded with the present of a gold ornament or silver money, and he would be given a special title which would make him highly honoured for the rest of his life.

There was one potter called Foo, who desired most eagerly to make a vase so beautiful that he would be rewarded by the Princess. This was not so much because he wanted a gold ornament or silver coins, as because he wished to please Lo-Yen and see her smile in gratitude. For her beauty was known throughout the land, and her smile was considered to be so gracious that once you beheld it you remembered it for the rest of your days.

So Foo worked in his shed in a poor part of the city, moulding and turning from morning till night. But although he was so hard-working a potter, the truth is that he was clumsy. Sometimes his clay was too dry and broke in the firing. Sometimes it was too thick, so that his vases would not ring to the touch. Sometimes the shapes were ugly, or the glaze was too thick, or the bottom uneven, so that the vase would not stand straight. All the same, he cared little for failure, and worked away diligently, confident that one day he would make the vase which would win him the Princess's bright smile. He had little to live on, but he needed little; the vases that turned out to be failures – and there were plenty of those – were sold as common water-pots, so that Foo was never without the means to live.

Well, the fifth month had come round again, and Foo was resolved to try his luck. So wrapping up his best vase in an old shawl, he walked up to the palace. He found a great crowd of people assembled. There were musicians and scholars, as well as soldiers to keep the crowd in order, fine ladies and gentlemen who had come to see the contest, and, of course, a throng of potters who had brought their vases from all over the kingdom.

On a throne in the great hall of state sat the Princess, magnificently clothed in silken robes, with jewelled combs in her hair. Yet, for all her splendour, she looked simple and kind, as she waited for the competitors to enter. The judges sat beneath the throne at a long table covered with paper and ink and brushes for them to make notes. In front of them was a smaller table spread with a soft cloth on which the vases would be placed. Down the sides of the hall were seats for the audience – silk-covered chairs and couches for the nobles, rough benches for the ordinary people. At the door of the hall stood the first competitor, an old white-haired potter from the far south, who had tried for fifty years to win the prize. Beside him stood a marshal – that is, a man whose business it was to lead him forward and place his vase on the table ready for the chief musician to strike it with the little hammer.

Foo took his place among the other potters. The Princess nodded her head to the chief steward for silence, and the steward struck a great brass gong, and everybody was suddenly hushed. Then the marshal stepped forward and announced the name of the old potter, and the province from which he came. Slowly the old man carried his vase to the table in the centre, placed it on the soft covering and stood aside. The chief musician examined it for a moment, then struck one, two, three notes on its rounded side. There was a murmur of approval. The note was a fine one – soft, but very pure and sweet. The judges made marks on their papers, for not only was the beauty of the tone considered, but also the shape of the vase, its colour, and its general appearance.

For several hours the contest went on. Some of the vases were tall and slender, some squat and round; some were as white and soft-looking as a summer cloud, others were brightly coloured – jade-green, sky-blue, flame-red, or lemon-yellow. All were different and all had different notes. To hear some of them, you might have supposed that the note came up from the depths of a tranquil sea; others suggested a sunlit stream in the mountains; one recalled the note of a wood-pigeon on a June afternoon, another was sharp and clear like the noise of a pebble dropping into water. Some notes were long and died away slowly; others were loud and hollow and sharp, and lasted only for the twentieth part of a second.

The day was warm, and the contest went on as if it would never end. The judges covered sheets and sheets of paper with their figures. No one knew who would win. Poor Foo, squatting on the floor just inside the great hall, several times nearly went to sleep. But at last it was his turn. The marshal called out his name and the name of his province, and Foo stepped forward, nearly tripping over the end of the old shawl which had come loose from his precious vase. He reached the table without dropping it, and handed it to the marshal, who placed it on the centre of the table – not without a faint smile, for it was a clumsy-looking object after all the elegant productions that had been seen that day. Its shape was roundish but not very regular; its colour was a dull grey, with an uneven glaze; and it did not stand any too steadily. The people of Chen are very polite, and no one said anything about the appearance of Foo's vase, but most of them thought how clumsy and ill-contrived it was. The court musician took a step forward and struck it with his hammer. It gave no note at all, but a hollow, dead sound, like the sound made by an old cracked jar when a boy kicks a stone against it. Unable to believe his ears, the musician struck it again more loudly. It sounded even worse than before. He tried a third time, more softly, and on the other side of the vase. It was no better. There was a pained silence among the onlookers, except for one little girl who was unable to keep herself from uttering a high-pitched laugh of sheer amusement. Her parents quickly silenced her, but they could scarcely help laughing. Afterwards everybody told each other that it was probably the worst vase that had ever been brought into the presence of the Princess. As for Lo-Yen herself, she said nothing, but looked a little sad.

There were no more vases, and the judges, after talking and comparing notes for some time, finally awarded first place to the old potter whose vase had been tried at the beginning. Everyone was pleased, for he had tried for many years, and now at last the Princess had smiled upon him and given him a tiny golden vase in exchange for his own vase of shapely white porcelain whose note was like the sound of the sea on the rocks in a little bay surrounded by tall cliffs. Then everyone went home, and Foo took up his clay pot, wrapped it in its shawl and went back to his shed.

He wasted no time feeling sorry about his failure, but the very next day began all over again. A year went by, and he had made no fewer than a hundred and fifty more pots, of all shapes and sizes. He had little ear for music, but when the fifth month came round again, he chose the one that seemed to him the best, and once more set off for the palace.

Once more the Princess sat on her throne surrounded by the nobles, the musicians and the judges; once more the marshals called out the names of the potters, and the chief musician tried out the music of every vase that was brought.

When it was Foo's turn, he came forward with his new vase wrapped in the same ancient shawl that he had used the year before. Some people recognized him, and could not help smiling to remember what a fool he had made of himself. This time he was a little nervous, for he did so want to please the Princess. Even if he did not win the first prize, he hoped that at least she would keep his vase in her collection and, when she was tired of all her other music, would request her musicians to play on his vase.

Well, sad to say, the noise made by the new one was even worse than that made by the old one.

'It is like the last cluck of a dying hen,' said one listener, and almost half the people could not help laughing out loud.

Without waiting for the end of the contest, Foo, covered with shame and blushing deeply, took up his vase and ran from the hall.

'At least I gave them a good laugh,' he said to himself. But he had noticed that the Princess did not even smile. She was too polite to do that, but she could not keep a certain look of pity from her face.

'Why does such a fool as that come a second time?' asked the chief musician, but no one could answer him. As for the judges, they did not even bother to put a single mark against Foo's name.

'Third time lucky,' said the clumsy potter to himself next morning, beginning all over again with a new barrel of clay. But somehow he seemed to make no progress at all. Some of his pots cracked before he could bake them; some fell to pieces in the oven; others were so misshapen that even Foo could see they were no good and would not even fetch a single small coin in the market.

It was as if he had lost heart. In the winter, he fell ill and had to spend much of his time keeping warm beside his wretched fire, and making soup from dried herbs to keep himself alive. When at last he felt better, he had scarcely enough spirit in him to begin work again. But one day spring came all in a rush. The sun shone clear and bright, the birds sang joyously, and flowers appeared on the trees in the city square. Foo sat down at his wheel and was soon turning away with a lighter heart than he had had for many months. But he could not think of making a vase for the contest. His landlord came for the rent, and the shopkeepers asked him for money for rice and other things he needed for his scanty meals. He had to work for a living, in order to make up for the time he had lost during his illness. When the fifth month came, Foo had not a single vase on his shelf – no, not so much as a flat dish he could take to the palace. But on the day before the contest he decided he must have one last try. He remembered the smile of the Princess two years before, when she had handed the old potter his reward, passing to him the little gold vase in a hand more white, more slim and shapely than anything he had ever seen. So with the image of the Princess in his mind, he seized a great lump of red clay and slapped it on to his wheel. He began to turn and shape and mould, until at last he could do no more. He had scarcely time to bake the pot hard before the contest began. He made the oven as hot as he dared and put the pot inside. He knew that he was firing it too fast, but he would have to risk that. All night long he sat beside the oven, keeping it hot by putting pieces of charcoal on the fire beneath. Then as dawn came, he let the fire die down, and opened the door of the oven. By this time the contest was due to begin, so as soon as the vase was cool enough he wrapped it in the old shawl without even troubling to look at it, and carried it to the palace.

Now, there was a new law about this contest, that if any potter tried for a third time, and utterly failed to satisfy the judges, he was to be thrown in prison until it was decided whether he would be kept there for the rest of his life, sent out of the country, or even put to death. It was a cruel law, and few potters dared risk a third attempt unless they had shown themselves reasonably competent in earlier contests.

No one supposed that Foo would have a third try. It would mean certain imprisonment, and several people, who felt kindly towards Foo, clumsy and pig-headed as he seemed, warned him of his danger.

'What do I care about prison?' he said. 'I've never been there before. I'm willing to try it.'

It was no use arguing. Foo was determined to make a fool of himself for the third time. As he looked through the door of the great hall towards where Lo-Yen was sitting, he cared for nothing else. Yet, as the contest went on, he could not help becoming dreadfully nervous, not because of the thought of going to prison, but because he seemed to have lost all hope of pleasing the Princess. Still, he had come to have a last try, and nothing would stop him now. By the time his name was called, poor Foo was trembling all over with fear.

He stepped forward, letting the shawl slip from his vase; and as he did so, he stumbled towards the centre of the hall, tripped over, and fell to the ground. He managed to hold his vase on high just long enough for everyone to see that it was even more monstrous and clumsy than the ones he had brought before. It really was a hideous affair – squat, pot-bellied, and with two rounded handles that were meant to be alike but which anyone could see didn't match. A great roar of laughter filled the hall, and in the middle of it could be heard the crash of Foo's jar as it fell on the marble floor and was smashed to pieces. Indeed, some even said it fell to pieces before it hit the floor.

'Take him away!' shouted the judges and the chief musician put his hands to his ears because he could not stand the uproar.

The Princess said nothing. Instantly, two or three guards ran forward, picked Foo up from the floor, and hurried him out of the hall. He was dragged from the palace and put in a dark dungeon, where he lay on the floor and wept from misery and weariness. Apart from his gaoler, who came at sundown and brought him a little rice and some water, everybody in the world soon forgot about him.

Meanwhile, a servant had come forward and swept up the pieces of Foo's wretched vase, and the contest went on. The prize was awarded to a young potter from the eastern province, on whom the Princess smiled enchantingly as she gave him a purse of white leather full of silver pieces in exchange for the exquisitely musical vase which he had brought.

Days passed, then weeks. Nobody thought about Foo, and even the gaoler almost forgot to bring him food and water. Nobody at the palace bothered to think what to do with him. As for Foo, he no longer cared whether he lived or died.

But a kitchen-boy, a mere youngster who ran errands for the palace cook, was fond of toys and loved playing about with odds and ends. He didn't care a rush if the cook called him a lazy rascal, so long as he had a length of string to make into a cat's cradle, or a piece of paper to turn into a boat and send down the stream when he had the afternoon off. At the time of the contest, he had seen the servant who swept up Foo's pot drop the bits into a rubbish-bin in the back yard. He noticed that as the bits of pottery dropped into the bin, they made a pleasant tinkling sound, rather like the rippling of a stream over the pebbles in some gravelly hillside. The boy picked the pieces out of the bin and took them away. He noticed that, as he tapped each piece, or dropped it on a stone floor, it made a different sound. So to amuse himself, he chipped a hole in each piece and threaded it on a string. Then he made a frame of bamboo sticks and hung the strings from it in a row. Next, he took a good-sized chicken-bone from the rubbish-bin and, using it as a hammer, began to fashion a little tune on the different bits of pottery. He found that the little pieces made high, tinkling sounds, and the bigger ones gave deeper notes.

Now the kitchen-boy, when he was not working, lived in a tiny room at the very top of the palace, just under the roof, and setting up his bamboo frame in the window, he spent hours tapping out little tunes on the broken crocks. You must remember that nothing like a tune had ever been heard before in the land of

Chen, so this was something entirely new. The kitchen-boy had a good ear for music, and it seemed to him that this new kind of sound, hopping up and down from low notes to high and back, was a merrier, more amusing kind of sound than just single notes.

Well, one afternoon, the Princess was walking on a terrace of flowering trees far below the kitchen-boy's window, and so quiet and still was the air that she heard the notes of the pottery instrument quite clearly. And so bright and merry was the kitchen-boy's tune that she gave a little laugh and almost danced for pleasure. At once she sent one of her maids upstairs to tell the boy to come down and bring with him whatever was making this strange new sound. Very shyly the boy came into the presence of the Princess and played his instrument for her until he could think of no more tunes, and it was long past time when he should have been helping the cook in the kitchen.

The Princess was delighted. She made the boy tell her how he had invented the instrument, and when he said he had got the pieces of crockery from the rubbish-bin, she wanted to know how they had come there. The boy could not remember, so the servants were sent for and questioned. At last the one who had swept up Foo's broken vase on the day of the contest remembered what had happened, and told the Princess.

'Yes, yes,' she cried, 'I remember! Poor fellow. I wonder what became of him.'

Well, to make a long tale shorter, the palace guards went to the prison where Foo was shut up, and brought him out. He staggered out, hardly able to walk for weakness and hardly able to see because the light was so strong after his dark cell. So he was carried to the presence of Lo-Yen, who thanked him most graciously for having made the pieces of crockery which had been turned into so delightful an instrument. Then he was given food and clean clothing, and afterwards was allowed to use a little shed in the palace yard, where he could go on making pieces of crockery for musical instruments. For soon this new music became the fashion, and the noble ladies and gentlemen all wanted sets of pieces strung on a bamboo frame. And the palace musicians came and learned the new music from the kitchen-boy, and invented different and complicated tunes of their own. And that was the beginning of true music in the land of Chen.

As for Foo, he got strong and well again, and worked happily at his trade in the palace yard. The Princess came and talked with him sometimes and smiled upon him; but to Foo she never smiled more sweetly than when she first spoke to him after he had left prison, and thanked him for making the vase that had broken in pieces.

The Cock, the Cat
and the Scythe

Old Matthew was a countryman living with his three sons in a cottage at the edge of a farm. He was very ancient and infirm. His eyes were dim, his voice weak, and his legs so feeble that before long he took to his bed. He had had a good life, though he had never saved any money. He was content to die, and only wished he had something to leave to his three sons, Peter, John and Colin.

When he knew that his time had come, he called the three boys to his bedside and said in a quavering voice, 'I must soon leave you, my sons, and I am sorry I have not much to give you. But what I have is yours. Peter, you shall have this fine

cock with his tall red comb and his feathers of green and gold.

'You, John,' went on the old man, 'shall have my cat. He is not much to look at, but he is a good mouser. No place where he stays shall ever be troubled with mice.'

John thanked the old man and took the cat. Then Matthew went on in his feeble voice, 'As for you, Colin, I have nothing to give you but my scythe. With it I have cut corn and mowed grass for many years. It is a good scythe. Take it, and may you have good luck. These things are not much, but take them to lands where they are not known, and you shall learn their true value.'

Then Matthew closed his eyes and fell asleep.

After the old man's death Peter took the cock and set out. But everywhere he went, he found that people had plenty of cocks and would give him nothing for such a common bird. In the towns he saw that the church spires had gold cocks upon them to tell which way the wind was blowing, and in the country every farmyard had at least one cock to wake the people every morning.

But Peter never gave up hope, and one day he reached an island where there were no cocks, and where no such bird had ever been seen. He showed the people the bird and said 'Look at him! See his tall red comb and his feathers of green and gold.'

'He is indeed splendid to look at,' said the people, 'but of what use is he?'

'He will wake you every morning at the same time,' said Peter. 'As it is, you never know when to get up. Some of you sleep so long that you waste the best part of the day. Besides, every night, at regular intervals, he crows three times. But if he crows during daylight, you shall know that there is to be a change in the weather. Believe me, there never was a more useful bird in the world.'

'You are right,' said the people, 'but is he for sale? How much do you want for him?'

'I must have a donkey laden with as much gold as it can carry.'

'Done!' said the people, who had plenty of gold. 'That is not much to pay for such a fine bird.'

So they gave Peter what he asked for, and off he went with his donkey laden with gold. Two great baskets it carried, and when Peter got home, his brothers were delighted.

'I too will go and make my fortune,' said John.

So off he went with the cat.

But everywhere he went the people had all the cats they needed – black cats, white cats, ginger cats and tabbies. They only laughed at John and told him to take his cat away and find something more useful. So off he went, till at last he came to an island where there were no cats. As you can imagine, the houses were overrun with mice. The people had done all they could to get rid of them, but still they came in their hundreds and ate up the corn and the cheese and the bread in their homes. No sooner had John let his cat loose than it caught a mouse, and then another and another and another, till everyone saw what a useful creature it was.

'That's not such a bad animal,' they said. 'It's not much to look at, but we can do with an animal like that. How much do you want for him?'

'I will let you have him,' said John, 'for as much gold as a horse can carry on its back.' They agreed that this was not much to pay for the cat, so they gladly gave John what he asked for. When John at last got home with his horse laden with gold, his brothers were overjoyed. It was now the turn of Colin to see what luck he would have. So one bright morning, he sharpened the scythe his father had left him, and set off into the world.

But everywhere he went, he found that the men carried scythes over their shoulders and went out each morning to cut the hay and the corn.

'Won't you buy my scythe?' he asked. 'It is a good scythe and used to belong to my father.'

'We can see that,' said the men, 'for it is a very old-fashioned scythe. We have better ones ourselves. Be off with you and see if you can find somebody who has never seen a scythe.'

Well, this was exactly what Colin did. One day he reached an island where no scythe had ever been seen. Yet the fields were full of ripe corn, and Colin waited to see how the people would harvest it. When the time came, he was amazed to see that they did not cut the corn down, but shot it down with cannons! All the guns on the island were brought out and fired off with tremendous noise and smoke. The farm animals were terrified; dogs barked, cats howled, and hens and geese were too frightened to lay. Nor was this a very good way of harvesting the corn, for some of it was shot near the top and the grain destroyed; some of the cannons fired right over the fields, and some of the cannon-balls were so hot that they set fire to the corn and burned it to the ground.

This was Colin's chance. He shouldered his scythe, and without noise or fuss cut down all the corn in one field before the people could get at it with the cannons. They were so pleased that they asked him how much he would take for his scythe.

'That's much better than guns,' they said. 'Such an invention is worth having.'

Colin told them they could have his scythe for a handcart full of gold, and this they gladly gave him. So off he went without his scythe but with a handcart of gold, which he pushed before him. When his brothers saw him, they were full of gladness. They prepared a noble feast to celebrate his home-coming, and afterwards they put all their money together and bought a big farm on which they worked in peace and friendship for many years. You can be sure of one thing – or rather, of three things. They bought themselves first a cock, to wake them in the morning, and next a cat, to keep down the mice in their barns. When harvest-time came round, they and their men worked with scythes to cut the corn, and never, never tried shooting it down with cannons.

The Discontented King

There was once a King who ruled over a pleasant country full of green hills, blue rivers and little busy towns. He lived in a square stone castle of medium size with tall stone towers, which the sun shone on from morning till night.

All round the castle was a park full of stately trees, and under the trees ran the King's deer that he sometimes hunted. The room where the King sat and signed papers and fixed his great red seal to them was a high sunny room, very warm and comfortable, overlooking a rose-garden, and beyond the rose-garden he could see the green park. Just outside the window was a tall spreading elm tree in which the white pigeons sat all day and made sweet cooing music. The King had a red robe with silver flowers on it and a great black horse for riding on when he travelled about his country. But still he was not happy. He was a discontented King, and it did not make things any better that he could not tell exactly why he was discontented.

The Queen was beautiful and graceful. She was nearly always cheerful and had a good temper. She was gay, amusing, and very fond of the King. She did not sit all day long on a silk sofa eating sweets and fanning herself, but was active and liked making things. She made cushion-covers and pillow-cases and long trailing gowns and tall elegant head-dresses. She liked riding about in the park too; but best of all she liked putting on her oldest dress and going into the kitchen when the chief cook was away and baking pastries and pies and sweetmeats and little sugar-rolls with cherries on top. She did not of course always wear her oldest dress. She had a blue robe with gold flowers on it, and a white horse for travelling round the country with the King. With such a Queen as his wife, the King ought to have been happy, but he was not. He was a discontented King, and it did not make it any better that he could not tell exactly why he was discontented.

The King and Queen had one daughter, who was gay and happy like her mother, but was not so fond of sewing and cooking. Instead she liked sitting in her little room high up in one of the castle towers and gazing out over the green fields to where on clear days she could just see the sea. She did not do this all day. Sometimes she would read, and sometimes she would help her mother or father. Sometimes she would even help her mother when she went into the kitchen to cook; especially when she was baking the little sugar-rolls with cherries on top. Sometimes she was so happy that she sang like a blackbird. She had a green robe and a dappled grey pony for riding about the country on, beside her father and mother. With such a daughter for Princess, the King ought to have been happy, but he was not. He was a discontented King, and it did not make it any better that he did not exactly know why he was discontented.

One day the King was sitting alone in his special room. He had done his signing and sealing for the day and was looking out of the window across the green lawns. The white pigeons were cooing peacefully in the great elm tree. It was a beautiful day, but still he was not happy. The Queen was in the kitchen, making little square tarts with slices of orange in them; the Princess could be heard chirruping away like a blackbird as she combed her long yellow hair in her little room at the top of the tower. She looked out of the window from time to time, to where her father's black horse and her mother's white one and her own dappled grey pony were grazing in the big meadow.

In the kitchen the Queen had a feeling that the King was not very happy, so when she had put her little orange tarts in the oven, she went up to the Princess's room and asked her to come down and talk to the King. The Princess had by now finished combing her hair and had done it up in a gold net with small gold leaves round the edge of it. She stopped singing when her mother told her the King was not happy.

'Oh dear,' she sighed, 'is father not happy again?'

'I'm afraid not, my dear,' said the Queen. 'Let us go down and see if we can suggest something to cheer him up.'

They went down to the King's room and sat down one on each side of him.

'It is a beautiful day,' said the Queen. 'Would you like to go hunting?'

'You go,' said the King, not exactly rudely, for he was never rude to the Queen; but still he did not want to go hunting.

'Well, what about a game of draughts with the new set made of red and white ivory?' said the Princess. 'I love playing draughts.'

'Well, have a game with your mother,' said the King, not exactly rudely, for he was never rude to the Princess; but still he did not want to play draughts.

'What about a swim in the lake?' said the Queen.

'Let the fishes swim,' said the King. 'It is what they are for.'

'What about some music, father?' suggested the Princess. 'You know you love music, and you have not yet heard the three new trumpeters who have come from Bohemia to join the royal band.'

'I have heard them practising all the morning,' said the King. 'Three trumpeters cannot practise in a castle like this without *everybody* hearing them. Not that they are not very good trumpeters, but when you feel as I do, the last thing you want to hear is a trumpet. I am tired of music. As a matter of fact,' went on the King unhappily, 'I am tired of everything. I am tired of hunting, I am tired of signing papers, I am tired of playing games, and I am tired of music and dancing and all the things I used to like best.'

The Queen and the Princess both looked very sad and the Princess began to cry a little.

'Oh, my dears,' said the King, sorry to see the Princess's tears, 'I am not tired of you. Oh, not at all. But I am tired of everything else. Listen to those silly pigeons cooing in that tree. I am tired of them. Above all I am tired of this castle.'

'But it is a lovely castle,' said the Queen, who was thinking of her orange tarts baking in the kitchen, and all the shining pots and pans on the shelves.

'It is a beautiful castle,' said the Princess, who was thinking of her little room in the tower, where she kept all her books and her games and her clothes and the shining mirror and hairbrush and comb on her dressing-table.

The King got up and put one hand on the Queen's shoulder and the other hand on the Princess's.

'My dears,' he said, 'if you do not mind, we will leave this castle and find another one. The truth is, I am tired of it, and I shall not be happy as long as we are here. I am sorry if this distresses you, but it is the only thing to do. We shall go to-morrow, all three of us.'

The Queen and the Princess did not like this idea, but they said nothing. They knew it was of no use to argue when the King was feeling like this.

'You, my dear,' he said to the Queen, 'may take your sewing-basket and your favourite lady-in-waiting and a little serving-maid to help you if you want to cook. And you,' he said, turning to the Princess, 'may pack up some of your favourite belongings, and you shall have a room to yourself just like your own room here.'

So it was arranged. The Queen agreed because she was a cheerful and contented person who usually did as the King wished. Besides she wanted to get back to the kitchen to see to her little square tarts – which, indeed, were only just saved from burning. They were all to set off next morning. The Lord Chamberlain was to go on in front in order to take possession of any castle that the King might fancy and to turn out any people that might happen to be living there. He was to have a small army with him, just a few knights and men, in case of difficulty. It may not seem polite or kind to turn people out of their homes, but really most people are glad of a change, and it is considered an honour to have the King living in your house. That is why the army was a very small one. It was not thought likely that there would be any difficulty. The three trumpeters from Bohemia were also to go on ahead to announce the King's arrival.

The Queen took her waiting-lady and her serving-maid and some of her favourite things; and the Princess packed up her most treasured belongings, as the King had said. Next morning the King put on his red robe with the silver flowers on, and the Queen put on her robe of blue with the gold flowers, and the Princess put on her green robe. The King got up on his black horse, and the Queen got up on her white one, and the Princess got up on her dappled grey pony. The three trumpeters blew a cheerful blast on their three trumpets, and the Lord Chamberlain rode on ahead with the knights and men. The servants rode behind. It was a beautiful morning, and everyone chattered happily. As they went out of the gates into the park, the white pigeons were cooing gently and peacefully in the elm tree.

'Really,' said the Queen, 'this is not such a bad idea. Perhaps we all needed a change.'

'I'm so excited,' said the Princess. 'This is quite an adventure.'

And the King laughed and began to sing a little. This was so unusual that even the black horse wondered what had happened to his master. He neighed gladly, and so did the Queen's white horse and the Princess's dappled pony.

They rode on for two days, and on the third day the weather changed. It became cold and cloudy. They had reached the edge of the King's country and were now by the seashore. There was a big stone castle standing on the cliff just above the sea.

'This will do,' said the King. 'We will live here.'

The Chamberlain went to the owner of the castle, who was an old man living there with his wife and only a very few servants. The old man and his wife were very glad to move to a smaller house at the edge of their grounds. The three trumpeters blew a loud blast, and the King and Queen and all the others rode into the courtyard.

They soon made themselves comfortable. The King took as his state room a large hall overlooking the sea. The Queen had a pleasant room beside it, and was soon unpacking her sewing materials and other things with the help of her lady-in-waiting.

The Princess had a big room in the tower. It was not unlike her own room at home, but it was much larger and instead of overlooking the green fields it overlooked the stone courtyard.

The Lord Chamberlain and the knights also found themselves rooms, and the three trumpeters were told to practise their trumpeting near the stables, as far away from the King as they could get.

For a month they all lived together in the castle by the sea. Everyone was contented, even the King. He had found new forests to hunt in. He even went out in a boat and fished. The Queen had soon found her way to the kitchen. It was not such a good kitchen as her own and nothing like so clean. However, she and the servants set to work and turned it out, and before long she was cooking there as well as she had ever done at home. The Princess at first missed her view over the green park, but from her window over the courtyard she could see people coming and going, and this amused her. She carolled away in her big room, or read her books, or went down the steep little path to the sea and played on the sands.

Then one day the Queen noticed that the King was looking miserable. She and the Princess went and talked to him.

'What is wrong, my dear?' asked the Queen.

'I don't know,' said the King. 'One thing is certain. We must move from this castle. I don't like it and it doesn't suit me.'

'Is it the noise of the sea outside your window?' asked the Princess.

'Well, it's certainly very noisy,' said the King.

'We could change your room,' said the Queen, 'and give you one on the other side.'

'I don't think it's the noise of the sea altogether,' said the King. 'I just don't like the place. It's too large. Much too large. I ought to have known that to begin with. What on earth did you let me come to a great barracks of a place like this for?'

He was never exactly rude to the Queen, but this question was almost rude. He looked out of the window.

'There's something wrong with this place. I miss something, but I don't know what it is. At any rate I can't stay here a day longer.'

The Queen and the Princess would cheerfully have stayed there for another six months, but they knew it was no use arguing.

By next morning everything was packed up once more and off they all went. The Lord Chamberlain and the trumpeters went first, with the knights and men-at-arms. Then came the King in his red robe with the silver flowers on it, riding his black horse; and the Queen in her blue robe with the gold flowers, riding her white horse; and the Princess in her green robe on her dappled grey pony. Everyone felt cheerful. As for the waiting-women and servants, they were always glad of a change.

They rode on for two days and on the third day they came to a castle standing by the shore of a great blue lake.

'This will do,' said the King, riding up to the Lord Chamberlain. 'This is just what we want. Take it.'

The castle was not difficult to take, for the owner was away, and the only people in it were three or four old servants, who did not at all mind having the royal family to live there.

Once more they settled down. The King had a room overlooking the lake, and the Queen found herself another beside it. The Princess had a little room at the top. It overlooked the lake and she could see the swans floating gracefully on its surface. True her room was dark and rather bare, but she made it as comfortable as she could and was soon singing away as she combed her yellow hair.

The King liked the new castle.

'It's a nice size,' he said to the Queen. 'That other place was much too big. Can't think how we ever lived there a day, much less a month.'

The Queen agreed that the new castle was much smaller. The kitchen, indeed, was very small – too small if anything. There was scarcely room for all the pots and pans and jars and bowls and dishes and plates that a good kitchen must have. Still, she managed to make it more or less as she wanted, and was soon busy making some of the little sugar-rolls with cherries on top that the Princess loved so much.

'This place isn't going to be bad at all,' said the Princess.

'Of course it isn't,' said the King. 'I told you it was just what we were looking for. Such a nice size – not too big and not too small.'

Then he went down to a kind of pavilion by the lake, took off his red robe with the silver flowers on it and his other royal robes, and put on a bathing costume. Soon he was swimming peacefully in the lake, while the swans glided round.

The weather was fine, and for a month everything went on well. Then the Queen again noticed that the King did not look altogether happy. She went and spoke to the Princess.

'I'm afraid this may mean another move,' she said.

The King had indeed grown tired of swimming. He found the swans greedy and ill-tempered, beautiful as they were. He did not like playing draughts here any more than he had done at home. There was no creature in the neighbourhood worth hunting, and the noise of the three Bohemian trumpeters practising once more annoyed him.

He found the Queen in the kitchen.

'Why are you wearing that old dress?' he asked. 'You look dreadful in it.'

'Why, my love,' said the Queen, much surprised, 'you always say you like me best in this old dress, for then you know I am happy among my jars and dishes.'

'Nonsense,' said the King, not exactly rudely, for he never spoke to the Queen really rudely, but still he did not like her in her old cooking dress.

'Go and put on your blue robe with the gold flowers on it, for we must be moving.'

'What, again?' asked the Queen, pretending to be surprised.

'You really want us to move again?' asked the Princess, who had just come in.

Yes, the King insisted on setting out once more and next morning, for the third time, off they went. The Lord Chamberlain went in front with the knights and trumpeters, then came the Queen in her blue robe with the gold flowers, riding her white horse; and the King in his red robe with the silver flowers, riding his black horse; and the Princess in her green robe, riding her grey pony. Then came the waiting-women and the servants, who were laughing and chatting merrily, for they never minded a move.

For two days they travelled like this, and on the third day the weather became terribly hot. The Princess sang no more, the Queen lost her cheerful looks, and even the horses began to pant and grumble. There was no more laughing and joking among the servants. They came to a great bare desert covered with stones, and at the edge of it there was a castle.

'This will do,' said the King to the Lord Chamberlain. 'Take it.'

The Chamberlain said nothing, for he was much too hot to speak, and the trumpeters blew a feeble blast on their trumpets. In the castle lived a wicked knight with four fierce dogs, but the men-at-arms drove them out, and soon the King and his party were settled in the castle. The weather grew cooler. Everybody was soon happy again. The King and the knights rode their horses over the desert. The Queen embroidered a beautiful veil in her cool sewing room overlooking the garden. The Princess made herself comfortable in a little round room in a round tower at the top of the castle. The King had a handsome chamber over the main gateway, and there he would sit signing and sealing the important papers that came every day by a special messenger.

'Now this is not so bad,' he said. 'That other place was really too small, and the one before was much too big, but this one is just right.'

The Queen did not like to tell him that the kitchen was in such a state that she had not the heart to do any cooking. Instead, she went back to her embroidery.

But the cool weather did not last long. In another month it was just as hot as ever. Once more the King became unhappy. He looked out of the window of his great state-room. There was something missing, but he did not know what it was. He was much too unhappy to do anything.

'What a miserable place this is!' he said to the Queen and the Princess one day. 'I really can't think how we ever came to settle here.'

'Why, it's very comfortable,' said the Princess, who had grown to be quite content with the castle at the edge of the desert. 'I have a lovely little room, and I can watch the queer creatures that come and play round the walls. My room is quite round, and I have never had a round room before.'

The King took no notice, but said to the Queen:

'Why are you always wearing your best robe nowadays? Why do I never see you in that homely old dress you use for cooking?'

The Queen did not like to tell him that she could do no cooking because the kitchen was so inconvenient, so she said nothing.

'All the same,' said the King, 'you'd better keep it on, for we must go travelling again. I couldn't stay another minute.'

He was not exactly rude to the Queen, for he was never quite rude to her, but he spoke very sharply all the same.

Well, off they set once more in the hot, hot weather. The Lord Chamberlain went first, very hot in all his Chamberlain's robes, and the knights and the men-at-arms went with him. Then came the King in his red robe with the silver flowers, and the Queen in her blue robe with the gold flowers, and the Princess in her green robe, which she used for travelling about the kingdom. The King rode his black horse, and the Queen her white one, and the Princess her dappled grey pony. Then came the waiting-people and the servants, who were always glad of a change; they were not laughing and joking much, for the weather was terribly hot.

For two days they rode like this, and all the time the road ran uphill. The weather gradually became cooler, and this pleased the horses, which had grown very tired. Presently they came to mountainous country, and just beyond a thick fir-wood they saw a handsome castle looking across a valley to a great range of snow-mountains.

The King called the Lord Chamberlain to him.

'Will it do, Your Majesty?' asked the Lord Chamberlain.

'It will,' answered the King. 'Take it.'

The castle in the mountains belonged to a knight who was away at the wars, and his lady was glad to leave it and go and live with her parents for a time, as she had become very lonely. So the three Bohemian trumpeters, who had grown skilful after all their months of practice, blew a splendid blast on their trumpets, and everyone rode into the courtyard.

'Now this is something like,' said the King. He chose himself a noble room on the first floor, and the Queen had a fine sitting-room beside it. The Princess once more climbed to the top of the castle, where she found herself a little room with a view towards the snow-mountains. They all settled down and life began once more. The Queen did not find things easy, for she had no more material for sewing. She had used it all up. The kitchen was small and there was no room for her as well as the cook who prepared the ordinary meals. The Princess had read all her books. The trumpeters practised no more, for they had become so skilful that they needed no more practice for the time being. The Queen and the Princess took to playing draughts with each other to pass the time away. They became used to the new life, and soon the Princess was chirping away as merrily as ever. The King went hunting wolves in the great black forest at the castle gates.

'A much better place than that dreadful old wicked knight's castle at the edge of the desert,' he said. 'And a lot better than those other two castles we tried.'

And they all agreed with him and hoped they would stay there some time.

Then it began to snow. Soon no more messengers could reach them because of the snow, so that the King had no papers to sign and seal. He had nothing at all to do, for there was no more hunting, and he was forced to join the knights and the men-at-arms in games of snowballing in the castle grounds. They snowballed each other in order to keep warm, for the weather continued very cold.

At the end of a month the Queen once more noticed that the King was looking unhappy. He was sitting in his state-room muffled up in his red robe with the silver flowers on it, and several other robes, one of them of fur, on top of it. He was looking discontentedly out of the window at the great black pine trees with their snow-laden branches. He felt that he ought to be happy. Yet there was something missing, though he could not tell what it was. He had often said he had too much work to do, and now he had none. All the same, he was unhappy.

'Of all the castles we have lived in,' said the King, 'this is the worst. What is the good, I ask you, of being stuck away in a place like this, where nobody visits us unless it is a lost wolf in search of a dead rat or a starving bird? The castle by the sea was bad enough, but it was better than this. So was the one by the lake, and so was the one by the desert. That was at least warm, but this is cold, cold, cold!'

The Queen said nothing. She and the waiting-woman had already packed up their belongings and were ready to go.

'And *draughty*!' the King went on. 'In all my life I have never lived in so draughty a place. Listen to the wind howling up and down these miserable cold passages. I can't stay here another minute – not another minute!'

'This time,' said the Queen, 'I really think we ought to go home. We've tried four castles already, and you haven't liked any of them.'

'Just as you like,' said the King. 'I don't care where we go so long as we get out of this draughty old ruin!'

'Hadn't we better wait till the snow melts and the weather's a bit warmer?' said the Queen.

'Certainly not. It will probably never melt. We must go at once, do you hear – at once!'

It was no use arguing. Once more everything was packed up, and they all set out. The King's red robe with the silver flowers was covered with a black fur cloak, and the Queen's blue robe with the gold flowers was covered with a brown fur cloak, and the Princess's green robe was covered with a white fur cloak. But how cold they all were! When they had gone a mile or two, the poor Princess was nearly weeping with the cold. The Queen was very sorry the King had made them all set off while the weather was cold, but she said nothing. Only she was determined that once they got home, nothing would make her leave it again in a hurry. Everyone was cold, and nobody chattered and laughed. The Chamberlain whistled to keep his spirits up, until the King told him to stop. The King was in a very bad temper. He was angry with the weather for being so cold, he was angry with the Queen for having allowed him to set out in such weather, and he was angry with himself for being so headstrong and discontented.

After some hours the wind blew stronger, and more snow began to fall. A terrible storm broke over them. They could no longer see which way they were going. They stumbled on as best they could. It was by now night time, and the moon, which ought to have been shining, was lost in the black storm. It was as much as they could do to keep together. The Princess was now crying piteously. There was nothing to do but struggle on. How the snow fell! How the wolves howled among the trees! How the wind blew in their faces and stung their cheeks!

'What a fool I have been!' said the King to himself. 'Why did I ever allow myself to leave home with my dear Queen and the poor little Princess? We shall never reach home alive, and it will all be my fault.'

But in the end, when they were tired out, and the horses could hardly go another step, the storm calmed down. The road had been going downhill steadily, and the weather became warmer. Although they did not know where they were, they knew they must be out of the mountains. When daylight came, they were in the middle of a thick mist. There was nothing to do but to go on until the mist cleared.

At last, in the middle of some open country dotted with trees, they saw a huge shape towering out of the mist. It was a castle. They could just make out its square shape and pointed towers. Everyone stopped.

'It will do,' said the King in a tired voice to the Chamberlain. 'Take it.'

Three blasts were sounded on the three trumpets, and the Chamberlain and the knights and men-at-arms rode forward through the mist.

Presently the Chamberlain came back to where the King sat on his horse waiting. He told the King that the castle had been left by its owners and was now in the hands of robbers.

'What a careless fellow the owner must be to leave his castle

like that!' said the King. 'Send in the men-at-arms and turn the
robbers out.'

The knights and the men-at-arms made short work of the
robbers. After half an hour's fighting the leader of the men-at-
arms came out and told the King that the robbers had been
driven off and were now lost in the mist. Once more the three
trumpeters sounded their trumpets, and the royal party rode
through the castle gateway. Then the mist began to clear. But
already the Queen had recognized her home.

Yes, it was really their old home. They had come upon it in the
mist without at first knowing it. Here they were at last, half dead
with hunger and tired out, at the very gates of their own castle.

But what a mess the robbers had left! Everything was dirty and
neglected. The furniture had not been polished, windows had
been broken and not mended, nothing had been cleaned or
washed for months.

After everybody had had a meal and a rest, the servants set to
work and made the place as tidy and comfortable as possible,

and it was not long before the King and the Queen and the Princess settled down to enjoy being at home again.

The Queen began to make cakes in her own kitchen, and to embroider and sew as she used to; the Princess was overjoyed to have her own little room in the tower overlooking the green park, and soon she was singing away and combing her hair as if she had never been away for a day, let alone several months.

As for the King, a whole pile of important papers arrived that very evening, and all these needed signing and sealing, so that he had work for a week. After all, he thought, as he sat down to his table and began work, home was not so bad, and all he had wanted was a little change. Then he looked up and listened to something he could hear outside the high window. The sun was shining. Far away in the meadow his own black horse and the Queen's white one and the Princess's dappled grey pony were feeding contentedly. Near at hand, the great elm tree spread its shady branches over the garden. The sound that had caught the King's ear was the cooing of the white pigeons in its leaves. What a peaceful, contented sound it was! That was what had been missing in all the other castles he had been to. There had been no cooing pigeons in the castle by the sea, or the castle by the lake, or the castle beside the desert, or the castle in the mountains. No, only in his own castle could he hear the peaceful noise of these contented birds. How wrong he had been to think the noise silly! It was the pleasantest noise in all the world, except for two – one was the talking of the Queen, who was nearly always good-humoured and cheerful, and the other was the singing of his little Princess as she combed her hair in the room upstairs in the tower.

When he had finished his work for the day, he sent for the Princess and asked her to play a game of draughts with him, and the Queen brought in some fresh orange tarts and some sugar-rolls with cherries on top. It was the happiest time they had spent since the King made them all set out on their long journey.

The Travelling Band

Have you ever heard of a band of travelling animals? No, not a circus – a real travelling band. Well, the story starts with an old donkey who was afraid his master would get rid of him. One day he overheard the farmer say to himself, 'I'll have to get rid of that donkey. He's too old and feeble to pull a cart any more, and he's not worth the food he eats.'

The donkey thought this cruel, for had he not worked faithfully for many years, and what did it cost his master to let him eat thistles at the end of the yard?

'I know what I'll do,' said the donkey to himself. 'I'll start a travelling band. I can make a fine noise, just like some of those trumpeters I've heard when the soldiers are passing. That's what I'll do.'

So one fine morning he kicked up his heels as best he could and went off down the lane at a comfortable trot. He hadn't been on the road long before he met an old hound.

'Good morning,' said the donkey. 'You look pretty miserable. What's the matter?'

The old hound snuffled and wheezed, and then he said 'I'm not long for this world. My master is a huntsman, and I heard him tell the stableman he'd have to get rid of me. Says I'm too slow for hunting and not worth the meat I eat – though goodness knows that's little enough.'

The poor dog's face and ears hung down as if he was going to cry, and his tail drooped between his legs as if he had never wagged it in his life.

'Can you bark?' asked the donkey. 'Give us a taste of your voice.'

The hound lifted up his head, opened his mouth and uttered a long mournful cry.

'Why, that's splendid!' said the donkey. 'You're just the fellow I need. Come along and join my band. People will travel miles to hear musicians like us. What with my bray and your bark, we'll be earning our living in no time.'

So the hound joined the donkey and together they trotted along the road. Very soon they met an old tabby cat with a face like three rainy days.

'What's wrong with you?' asked the donkey.

The cat gave a melancholy miaou and said 'My mistress has driven me out. She says I'm getting blind and my teeth have fallen out, I'm no use for mousing any more. I'm not worth the milk I drink – that's what she says. But goodness knows it's little enough she gives me.'

'You can still give a fine catcall, I dare say,' said the donkey. 'Let's hear you.'

So the poor old cat lifted up her head, opened her toothless jaws and wailed as loud as she could.

'Why, that's fine. You're just the girl we're looking for. Come and join our band. What with my bray, the dog's bark and your operatic skill, we'll be as fine a band as any in the world.'

So off they went together. Before long they met a cock with a very doleful countenance. His tail feathers dragged along the ground and his comb was pale and drooping.

'What's wrong with you?' inquired the donkey. 'What are you doing all by yourself on the roads?'

'I've run away,' said the cock. 'Only thing to do. Master's got visitors coming on Sunday, and I heard him tell the cook to get me ready for the stewpot. How would you like that?'

'I've never heard of stewed donkey,' answered the donkey. 'But I've troubles of my own. Now you're just the fellow we want. I needn't ask if you're a musician, for everyone knows you are. How would you like to join our travelling band?'

The cock readily agreed, and crowed with pleasure. At this the cat began howling, the dog barked, and the donkey joined in with a loud 'Hee-haw!'

When they had all finished, the donkey said 'That's not half bad for a first try. We'll soon be earning our living at that rate.'

So off they went, all four of them, and as darkness came on, they found themselves in a forest. Here they prepared to spend the night. The donkey lay on the ground beneath a tree; the old hound curled up beside him; the cat climbed on to a branch, and the cock flew to the top of the tree. He looked round and soon made out with his keen eyes a glimmer of light from a cottage not far off.

'I think we'd be more comfortable over there,' he said. 'It's getting cold out here, and besides, we might find a bite to eat.'

Now the cottage belonged to a robber band, who, just at that moment, were sitting down to supper after a hard day's burglary. The donkey looked in at the window and saw them as they sat round a table in a room where a warm fire was burning.

'Let's give them some music,' said the donkey. 'Then perhaps they'll let us come in and give us something to eat.'

So the donkey stood under the window, the hound got up on his back, the cat climbed on to the hound and the cock perched himself on top of the cat.

'Now then,' said the donkey. 'Let's surprise them. One! two! three! four!'

Then immediately they all made as much noise as they could.

The donkey brayed, the hound barked, the cat miaoued and the cock crowed as if it was the day of judgement. At this terrible sound the robbers dropped their knives, jumped up from the table and rushed out of doors into the woods. They thought they had been suprised by demons or witches, so they went and hid in the bushes as fast as their legs would take them. At this moment the donkey broke the window, and all the animals jumped into the warm room and fell to with a will on the food laid out on the table. They ate everything they could find, for they were all hungry and none had eaten a square meal since leaving home.

When they had had enough, they blew out the lights and settled down for the night. The cat stretched herself on the hearth; the hound lay by the door; the cock perched on a beam overhead, while the donkey went out into the yard.

At last, when all was quiet and the fire had died down so that the cottage was in darkness, the robbers crept back, and the bravest of them tiptoed inside. Seeing the two bright eyes of the cat on the hearth, he mistook them for the last sparks of the fire. So he took a taper from his pocket and held it towards the cat, to get a light for the candles. At once the cat screamed at the robber and spat at him fiercely. The robber, taken by surprise, ran from the cottage, and as he did so, the dog bit him in the ankle and the cock screamed 'Cock-a-doodle-do!' Then the donkey in the yard gave him a kick as he passed, so that by the time the robber got back to his companions, he was trembling with terror and hardly able to speak.

'The p-p-place is haunted,' he told his companions, as soon as he could make himself understood. 'There was an old w-w-witch by the fire who spat at me. A man was standing by the d-door and cut me in the leg with a knife. When I got outside, there was a black m-monster who hit me with a wooden club. And there was a demon who had turned himself into a cock and was shouting "Cut the devil in two!" I'm not going back into that house, not if you give me all the gold we've ever taken.'

Well, none of the robbers dared go back into the cottage, so the animals' travelling band took possession of it. There they settled down to live peacefully together. They practised their music, and nobody troubled them, as the cottage was believed to be haunted. When they ran short of food, off they went together and performed at fairs and markets. Soon they became famous and were never again without a roof over their heads and money to buy food with.

GHOSTS THAT HAUNT YOU
ed. Aidan Chambers

Bumps, squeaks and terror in the moonlight. Sometimes funny, sometimes horrifying, this superb collection of spooky stories all involve children in some way.

A CHRISTMAS CARD
Paul Theroux

A wonderfully eerie story! Driving down from the city, parents and two young boys go hopelessly astray in the snow and dark, but at last they find welcoming shelter for the night in a strange old mansion. 'This place is so far from anywhere that you have to be lost before you find it,' said their host, a tall man in a cloak. He is nowhere to be seen when they leave in the morning but he has left them a card – and it is the boy Marcel who first perceives that this card is a kind of map, what's more a *living* map.

THE DRIFTWAY
Penelope Lively

The Driftway is a strange road, a travelling road, centuries old. For those who choose to hear them, there are messages along the Driftway – echoes from the past. On the run from home with his little sister, Paul thumbs a lift on old Bill's horse-drawn cart, but as they slowly travel down the Driftway the messages come and Paul begins to see something special for him in each one. A fascinating and strangely haunting novel.

KEPT IN THE DARK
Nina Bawden

Clara and Bosie and Noel all found the big strange isolated house and the grandparents they'd never met before rather daunting. And when David turned up and claimed he belonged there too, things got even more disturbing. There were so many secrets to find the answers to.

THE CLOCK TOWER GHOST
Gene Kemp

Addlesbury Tower is haunted by Rich King Cole, a mean old man who fell off it long ago in mysterious circumstances. Its newest terror is Mandy – feared by her family and eventually by the ghost too. In the war they wage to dominate the tower, Mandy and King Cole do frightful and funny things to each other, little guessing how much they really have in common.

THE GHOST OF THOMAS KEMPE
Penelope Lively

Strange messages, fearful noises and all kinds of jiggery-pokery! It began to dawn on James that there was probably a ghost in the house. But what kind of ghost was it that had come to plague the Harrison family in their lovely old cottage? James sets out to find the answer in this delightfully funny story.

GHOSTS, SPOOKS AND SPECTRES
ed. Charles Molin

From the pens of Charles Dickens, H. G. Wells, James Thurber, Sir Arthur Conan Doyle and many other master storytellers, come these phantoms of the night, bringing secrets from beyond the grave. Eighteen tales – some disturbing, some amusing and some downright terrifying!

THE GHOST DOWNSTAIRS
Leon Garfield

Mr Fast signs away the last seven years of his life in return for the riches of the world – but gets more than he bargained for!

THE GHOST'S COMPANION
ed. Peter Haining

Thrilling ghost stories by well-known writers – and the incidents which first gave them the idea.

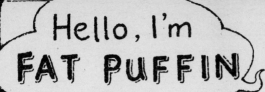